THE BUCKTAILS:

PERILS ON THE PENINSULA

by

William P. Robertson & David Rimer

ISBN 0-7414-3348-6

Published by:

INFIN∞ITY
PUBLISHING.COM

*1094 New DeHaven Street, Suite 100
West Conshohocken, PA 19428-2713
Info@buybooksontheweb.com
www.buybooksontheweb.com
Toll-free (877) BUY BOOK
Local Phone (610) 941-9999
Fax (610) 941-9959*

Printed in the United States of America

Printed on Recycled Paper

Published August 2006

CONTENTS

AUTHORS' NOTE

In writing our series of Bucktail novels, we discovered a peculiarity in the history of the regiment. In the spring of 1862, the First Pennsylvania Rifles was divided into two brigades to take advantage of their outstanding skirmishing and scouting abilities. Companies C, G, H, and I under Lieutenant Colonel Thomas Kane were sent with Bayard's Flying Brigade to catch Stonewall Jackson in the Shenandoah Valley. Meanwhile, Companies A, B, D, E, F, and K were placed under the command of Major Roy Stone and sent to the Virginia Peninsula. Because our other novels followed Kane's men, a void was left in the Bucktails' history. Perils on the Peninsula was written to fill that void with an active and accurate account of Stone's riflemen.

To ensure that Perils complimented our series, we further developed the character of Joe Keener of Company K, who appears in The Bucktails' Shenandoah March and The Bucktails' Antietam Trials. We also introduced the young soldiers Jack, Jude, and Zack Swift to provide characters with whom our juvenile audience could identify. Letters between Keener and Sergeant Hosea Curtis of Company I and cameo appearances by Curtis, Boone Crossmire, Bucky Culp, and Jimmy Jewett also help establish the connection to our other books.

The full adventures of the Company I Bucktails can be found in Hayfoot, Strawfoot: The Bucktail Recruits, The Bucktails' Shenandoah March, The Bucktails' Antietam Trials, The Battling Bucktails at Fredericksburg, The Bucktails at the Devil's Den, and The Bucktails' Last Call.

ACKNOWLEDGMENTS

The authors would like to thank the many dedicated Civil War reenactors who helped bring this story to life. On the front cover Robert Burns portrays a Bucktail skirmisher. Special thanks are also due to Marcia Rimer, Josie Copello, Gary Grove, and Tom Aaron for helping with the research. All photos were taken by William P. Robertson unless otherwise noted. Robertson's author photo and the back cover photo were provided by Nola Fox. David Rimer's author photo is courtesy of Marcia Rimer. This book is dedicated to the fighting spirit of the Company K Bucktails of Clearfield County.

Daniel Blett, pictured above, was an actual Bucktail soldier. He was 33 years old when he enlisted and served as drillmaster for Company K. He transferred to Company F and was promoted to first sergeant and then to second lieutenant. Daniel sent this photo to his son, William. It is used courtesy of Dr. Gary Grove, who is the great, great, great grandson of Blett.

BUCKTAILS' ROUTE TO WAR JUNE-SEPTEMBER 1862

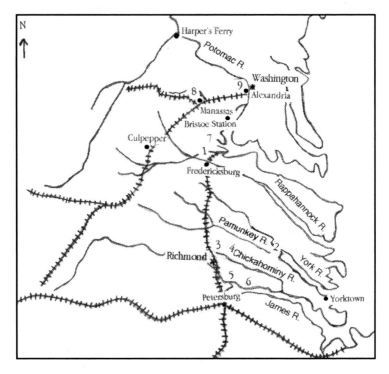

1. The Bucktails under the command of Major Roy Stone leave their camp at Falmouth, VA, on June 8, 1862.
2. The Bucktails are taken by steamer up the York River to White House, VA-- General George B. McClellan's supply base. The First Rifles arrive on June 11.
3. On June 26 Company K under Captain Edward Irvin are taken prisoner west of Mechanicsville. At Beaver Dam Creek east of Mechanicsville Companies A, B, D, E & F hold off the Rebels.
4. At Gaines' Mill on June 27 the Bucktails help stymie the Rebs until the Union Army withdraws across the Chickahominy River.
5. The Bucktails watch the Union artillery batter Robert E. Lee's forces at Malvern Hill on July 1, 1862.
6. The Bucktails rest and refit at McClellan's new base at Harrison's Landing on the James River from July 2-August 14.
7. The Bucktails are taken by steamer to Aquia Creek to begin a new campaign against the Rebels. They arrive on August 20.
8. The Bucktails participate in the Second Battle of Bull Run on August 28, 29 & 30.
9. Companies A, B, D, E, F & K under Colonel Hugh McNeil reunite with Companies C, G, H & I under Lieutenant Colonel Thomas Kane at Alexandria, VA on September 2, 1862.

CHAPTER ONE:
TWO HULKING YANKEES

Two hulking Yankees leaned heavily against a creaking, makeshift bar. They guzzled huge tankards of rotgut whiskey as they exchanged drunken banter. One of the giants was a sergeant with bulky muscles rippling beneath his blue sack coat. The other soldier had no stripes decorating the plain blue sleeves that housed his powerful biceps. That both men were of the same regiment was apparent by the deer tails sewn on their kepi caps.

The two Yankees also shared a common apprehension. As they pounded down the forty-rod, they kept glancing out the open door of the tavern at the deserted Falmouth street outside. Their nervousness, however, did little to lower the volume at which they shouted.

"I'm sure glad we got ta tip a few be-fore our regiment gits split up," thundered Hosea Curtis, the big sergeant.

"I jess hope Colonel Kane don't send no patrol down here ta ruin our little reunion," replied Private Keener, again peering warily past his friend.

"We'll jess have ta skedaddle if he does. Ain't no sheriff alive done ketched us yet, so I reckon no patrol's gonna do it neither."

Lifting his hat from an unruly shock of red hair, Joe fanned himself and then said, "This here liquor's made me hot e-nough already. I don't need no runnin' ta git the sweat streamin' down my back."

"Then we'll jess have ta stop at another pig's ear an' down us some home brew ta cool off. Ya know us Bucktails must be mighty fine sharpshooters if the brass needs ta de-ploy you ta the Peninsula with Major Stone while I's

1

marchin' ta the gol-dang Shenandoah Valley with Kane."

"I never heared o' no regiment bein' divided in the middle of a war," replied Keener. "Most generals don't like ta lose men under their command. We must be special, all right!"

"Well, at least that grand review we done taday fer President Lincoln was a real dandy! Ain't Old Abe somethin'? Dressed in his stovepipe hat, he even done towered over us boys."

"Yeah, seein' Lincoln was even better than the ruckus we caused in Smethport back in '59. Don't ya remember, Hosea, how we busted up that pig's ear, an' the barkeep went an' fetched the law?"

"Yeah, Joe!" laughed Sergeant Curtis. "When that gol-dang tin star arrived, he took one look at us an' run back the way he come ta lock hisself up in his own jail."

"Good thing, too," chortled Private Keener, "or we'da grabbed his legs an' used 'im fer a wishbone!"

"We sure had us some big times, all right, 'tween fightin' all comers an' loggin' them mountains o' McKean County. We'd git a crosscut saw movin' so fast, we caught more 'n' one tree on fire before we felled her!"

"Yeah, when we wasn't droppin' hemlocks er skiddin' 'em inta Potato Creek, we knew how ta have us some fun!"

"It's too bad ya had ta move down Clearfield way," sighed Curtis as he gave his pal a punch on the shoulder. "Then, we wouldn't have ta sneak off ta have us a farewell drink. You'd already be in Company I instead o' gol-dang Company K."

"Oh, the fellas I'm with ain't so bad," replied Keener, cuffing Hosea amiably with one of his big paws. "Captain Irvin's a straight fella, an' Sergeant Blett, who's a wise, old husband, takes good care o' our squad. We also gots the three Swift brothers that keeps things mighty lively, let me tell ya. How 'bout the boys you's servin' with?"

"The only real de-pendable private I got is Frank Crandall. He's serious as a preacher an' steady as one, too. I also got two babes I had ta wet-nurse in the beginnin'. One's a gol-dang half-breed Injun an' the other a sissy drummer boy. At Dranesville they proved their mettle, though, an' I reckon they'll be darn fine soldiers in the end. That is if they don't listen ta this cocky private named David Crossmire, who fancies hisself a regl'ar joker. We all calls 'im 'Boone' 'cause he's always crowin' 'bout how he can shoot like old Dani'l hisself."

"Well, he wouldn't be a Bucktail if he couldn't hold his own with a rifle," slurred Joe. "I reckon the finest marksmen in the whole U.S. Army comes from the Wildcat District o' good old Pennsylvany!"

"Pennsylvania?" scoffed a lanky, cold-eyed sergeant, striding into the tavern with a full squad of men dressed in green uniforms at his back. "The only men who can really handle a weapon joined up with me in Berdan's Sharpshooters!"

Berdan's men streamed purposefully into the tavern and encircled the two drunken Bucktails. They were obviously on patrol, carrying Sharps rifles slung over their shoulders. The soldiers had a hungry look about them as if they'd run out of rations days ago. Their keen eyes peered disapprovingly at Hosea and Joe until their corporal growled, "Don't you think we ought to run these lushes in, Sergeant?"

"You ain't got no authority over us Bucktails!" snapped Curtis.

"That doesn't keep us from being disgusted by you," mocked the other sergeant. "No true marksman would abuse his body like you fellows. It takes real discipline for a man to master his weapon and shoot it consistently."

"Well, 'cuse me fer breathin' the same air," muttered Joe. "If you carried muskets instead o' them fancy breechloaders, I reckon ya wouldn't act so high an' mighty."

"We earned the right to carry these Sharps," spat the corporal. "We're in the regular army, not a bunch of backwoods reserves like you."

"It don't matter what guns ya fire," growled Curtis. "If I hadn't. . . fergot. . . my Springfield back at camp, I'd match ya shot fer shot."

3

"Of whiskey, maybe," sneered the Berdan sergeant with a derisive laugh.

"Well, yer lordship, if ya hate drinkin' so much whatcha doin' in this here tavern?"

"Stamping out bar rats like you."

"Oh yeah?" replied Hosea dangerously. "I don't reckon you'd be talkin' so big if it weren't ten o' you 'gainst Joe an' me."

"It's no wonder you Bucktails got banned from the Harrisburg city limits for brawling. You are a disgrace to the uniform of a U.S. soldier!"

The insult had barely left the Berdan sergeant's lips when Curtis' big fist smashed them to jam. Spitting blood and broken teeth, the lanky soldier reeled and then came at Hosea swinging wildly. He unleashed a whirlwind of punches that Curtis blocked or ducked. Next, he jabbed for the gut, only to be thwarted. He became so busy flailing his fists that he forgot the Bucktail could hit back. Hosea laid him out with an uppercut to the jaw that sent the Berdan sergeant flying across the barroom. He landed on a rickety table, smashing it to kindling. Groaning heavily, he lay amid the wreckage sinking in and out of consciousness.

While Hosea was contending with the sergeant, one-by-one the other green coats leaped at Keener, only to be hurled to the floor by the hulking giant. The first to recover was the obnoxious corporal. He shook his head, dusted himself off, and danced toward Joe, sparring like a professional boxer. Repeatedly, he juked and jabbed, but the blows he landed stung his fist more than they hurt his opponent. In frustration, he snatched up his rifle and swung the butt end at Joe's noggin, knocking off his bucktailed cap. Emitting a low growl, Keener grabbed the corporal and gave him a head butt that shattered his nose. Blood squirted everywhere, drenching the other U.S. Sharpshooters that now pressed forward to renew the fight.

Still outnumbered eight to one, Keener roared like a cornered bear. He grabbed a scrawny private and smashed him like a rag doll against the nearest wall. Another Berdan man leaped on his back, and Joe whirled around and around trying to free himself from the other's choke hold. Finally, he banged his rider against a sharp corner of the bar until the fellow squealed and let go. Immediately, two more green coats pounced on him. He lifted the lean soldiers off their feet and banged them together until their teeth rattled and their heads threatened to snap off their necks. When he released them, the bloodied soldiers slid limply from his powerful grasp to rise no more.

Meanwhile, Hosea knocked down a charging Sharp-shooter with a blow to the windpipe. Another he tossed through a window. His remaining two assailants rushed him from opposite corners of the room. With an agility that belied his size, Joe juked out of the way at the last second. The two Berdan men crashed together, knocking themselves out. This brought a jarring conclusion to the hostilities. Hosea and Joe grinned at each other and made for the unbroken bottles of whiskey behind the bar.

Curtis and Keener had little time to relish their victory, for the next instant brought the sound of patrol whistles and running feet from outside. Leaping through a shattered side door that hung from one hinge, the Bucktails loped up an alley and onto the caisson-rutted road that led to their camp. The riflemen glanced apprehensively back down the winding streets of Falmouth before tearing along the northern bank of the churning Rappahannock River. A mile and a half fairly melted beneath their flying feet, even though no soldiers pursued them.

The Bucktails never slowed until they passed a row of tall cedars that bordered a splendidly kept parade grounds. Beyond this groomed field, they ducked their hulking frames through the evergreen arch that announced the entrance to the Union camp. Every tent opening had a bower of pine boughs over it, too, and the strong scent of evergreen helped mask the stench of whiskey that emanated from the soldiers' blood and liquor stained uniforms.

Hosea and Joe lurched along until they came to the statue of a huge evergreen buck sporting an actual deer tail.

Behind this statue stretched the company streets of the Bucktail Regiment.

"Well, good luck to ya, Joe," said Curtis, extending a huge paw to his friend.

"Yeah, I reckon we'll be con-fined ta camp after ta-day," grinned Keener, shaking Hosea's hand. "Wouldn't be the first time."

"Maybe Berdan's rascals will be too embarrassed ta squeal."

"Hope so, Hosea. Keep yer powder dry. See ya when I see ya."

"Hey, an' stay in touch. I kin gol-dang read ya know!"

"See ya. I'll drop ya a line er two. You betcha! Tell that Boone fella 'hello'. If he gits too cocky, I'll helps ya put 'im in his place, sure as shootin'."

Keener waved a last goodbye, ducked through the evergreen arch over the Company K street, and lumbered toward a squad of Bucktails gathered around a cauldron of bubbling stew. With a lopsided grin, Joe said, "Is that all you stinkin' fellas do is eat? The way you's droolin' over that slop, you'd think it were a haunch o' venison er yer mama's hasty puddin'."

"What in the devil happened to you?" whistled a mid-dle-aged sergeant with a well-trimmed goatee. "It looks like the whole Reb army danced on your face."

"Ain't none o' my blood there, Sergeant Blett," chor-tled Keener. "It come from a fancy pants Berdan fella that somehow lost his balance an' bumped his nose on my head."

"Musta been an awful tall fella ta have done that," chuckled a wiry private with what looked like a saber cut across his cheek. The private had a broad, oval face topped by close-cropped brown hair. Very white teeth gleamed in his wide-set mouth when he laughed.

"No, Zack, he were more clumsy than tall."

"Well, you best git cleaned up be-fore Captain Irvin sees ya," warned a second private, who could have been Zack's twin if he'd have been five years older. Although barely thirteen, the lad wore the air of a veteran like a badge.

6

"That's good ad-vice, Jack," said the middle Swift brother, Jude, leaping up to splash some water on a handkerchief from his canteen. "Here. Quick!"

Just as Keener snatched the dripping handkerchief from Jude's hand, a young captain ducked hatless from his wall tent and proceeded up the company street directly toward Sergeant Blett's squad. Edward Irvin was a graduate of Princeton and carried himself like the gentleman he was. He wore his thick hair parted on the side and sported a beard on the very tip of his chin. He had an engaging smile when he chose to display it, but that wouldn't be today.

"Where in tarnation have you been?" exploded Captain Irvin when he spotted Keener crouching with the others around the smoking fire pit.

"Nowhere. . . special, sir," sputtered Joe, hunkering as low to the ground as a monster of his size could.

"Then why are you skulking there with blood splattered all over your face? And don't say you cut yourself <u>shaving</u>. An unkempt rascal like you wouldn't know the meaning of that word."

"No, sir, I. . . um. . . was de-fendin' the honor o' the Bucktails ag'in a whole squad o' Berdan's Sharpshooters. They was de-famin' us Pennsylvania boys, sir, an' I had ta set 'em straight."

"Yeah, by making their noses crooked," replied Irvin with a knowing shake of his head. "It's a good thing you didn't lie to me, Private, because I just heard how you and Hosea Curtis busted up the Falmouth Tavern. I've been ordered to send half of your next pay to the owners who suffered the damage. That should make you think twice before sneaking off for a snort of popskull."

"Yes, sir."

"Although I don't care much for those high privates in Berdan's outfit, I don't condone brawling with them either. I'll see what I can do to defuse the tension between our regiments."

"Thank you, Captain, sir," said Keener meekly.

"All right, then," continued Irvin, "I want you men to

7

turn in right after supper. We've got a tough campaign ahead of us, and we'll need all the rest we can get to be ready for it. I don't know about you, but I'm tired of hearing about those other regiments hogging all the glory on the Peninsula. Our chance is coming soon the way General McClellan keeps screaming for reinforcements. I pray every night that we'll be summoned to battle, so the Bucktails can be the first to march into Richmond."

"You said a mouthful there, sir," thundered Sergeant Blett, his dark eyes glistening. "Let's hear it for the Bucktails, the grandest regiment in Little Mac's whole army. Hip, Hip, Hurrah! Hip, Hip, Hurrah! Hip, Hip, Hurrah!"

CHAPTER TWO:
ON TO THE PENINSULA

In the morning Joe Keener exhaled a great groan when the shrilling of bugles roused him from his blanket just after first light. His head was throbbing from all the liquor he had sucked down with his pal Curtis. Now, he was faced with the prospects of fighting a pounding headache while marching all day in the withering sun.

Noting Keener's pained expression, Sergeant Blett said, "Looks like someone has a brick in his hat."

"Ain't no room fer a brick," grunted Joe. "There's already an elephant squeezed in there."

"Probably lookin' fer that peanut you call a brain," chuckled Zack Swift.

"Now, Jack, do ya see why we keep warnin' ya to stay away from forty-rod an' such?" declared Jude to his younger brother.

"Yeah," replied the lad, scurrying to gather up his gear. "Havin' Joe around reminds me o' lots o' things I shouldn't do."

"What do ya mean?" protested Keener sourly. "I already taught ya plenty 'bout fightin' the Rebs, kid."

"If you don't get him fighting the same demons as you, I'm sure your lessons in warfare will help him plenty," said Sergeant Blett, winking at Jack. "You're a real scrapper, Keener, when you're not brought down by your own excesses. Let's get going, boys. We don't want to be late for assembly. Maybe this is the day our orders will finally come through. I'd be just as happy staying right here, but I know how much the rest of you love the rebel yell and the sound of bumblebees."

The Bucktails scrambled for the parade grounds still pulling on their jackets and haversacks. When the whole regiment had rushed into formation, Lieutenant Colonel Thomas Kane rode a rawboned war-horse onto the field to inspect the riflemen. Kane was a jockey-sized officer with a bushy, black beard and intense eyes. The respect his men held for him was evident by the way they had snapped to attention at the first sight of his charger trotting from headquarters.

Keener, who stood at attention in the front rank, noted the fresh, red scar that Kane's facial hair did not quite cover and nodded approvingly at his commander. That fella might not be bigger than a tick on a bayin' hound, but he sure got grit, reflected Joe. The way he shook off gettin' shot in the face at Dranesville, he must eat Minie balls fer breakfast!

After Colonel Kane cantered back and forth for one final inspection of the regiment that had been his creation, he ordered Companies C, G, H, and I to step forward and form up on the road. Following a brisk salute to Major Roy Stone, Kane blared, "Okay, men, we're off to the Shenandoah where we'll prove once and for all that well-trained riflemen who are traveling light can outperform the best cavalry unit in Mr. Lincoln's Army. For months I've been teaching you men my special tactics, and now we've got just the mission to test our salt. At the double-quick, march!"

Companies A, B, D, E, F, and K stood watching their departing comrades shoulder their Springfield muskets and then jog along after Kane's mount. Keener had a hard time keeping a straight face when he saw the obviously hurting Sergeant Curtis stumble into motion and trot heavily through the swirling dust kicked up by 400 pairs of heavy brogans. Hosea vented his foul mood through a string of just audible curses hurled at the men of his squad. The soldiers who took the brunt of Curtis' wrath were a lanky, hawk-nosed private and his broad-faced, bespectacled friend, who couldn't have been more than thirteen years old.

Them must be the babes Hosea's been wet-nursing, thought Keener wryly. I reckon his tongue'll be crackin' at them two boys' rears like a black snake whip 'til they meets up with Johnny Reb.

After Kane's unit had disappeared in a distant cloud of red dust, Major Stone noted the disappointed looks shared by many in his six remaining companies of Bucktails. Drawing his medium height frame erect, Stone bellowed, "Time we do some drilling of our own, boys. We don't want to get too soft to help Little Mac when he needs us. Attention! Shoulder arms!"

The major then proceeded to lead his riflemen through a half-hour of the manual of arms followed by another two hours of marching and skirmishing drills. By the time the men were dismissed back to camp, Joe Keener was drenched with clammy sweat, and his face was flushed horribly.

"What did you do, Joe, sneak off and take a dip in the Rappahannock while we were drilling?" joked Sergeant Blett, noting Keener's soaked uniform.

"Smells more like he done slogged through a swamp," laughed a rangy private named Enos Conklin.

"Or rolled in some day-old home brew," needled the eldest Swift brother.

"Yeah, crack on me all ya want," muttered Joe, "while I's too weak ta de-fend myself. I suppose yer kin gots them bayonet tongues o' theirs sharpened, too."

"Not me," replied Jack Swift. "I think ya oughta go lay in the shade fer a while 'til yer color gits back ta normal."

"Yeah, we don't want ya joinin' Colonel McNeil in the Invalid Corps," added Jude Swift. "It's too bad how he come down with the fever an' will probably miss us takin' Richmond."

"If we ever gits called up," grumbled Conklin, scratching the dirty stubble he called a beard. "How in tarnation did Kane git so lucky ta see combat ag'in?"

"His money and influence did it," replied Blett. "Didn't you know that his brother is Elisha Kent Kane, the famous explorer?"

"An' I'm Father Christmas!" scoffed Keener.

"Well, any way you looks at it," concluded Jude,

"Kane's seceded an' taken half the dang regiment with 'im."

The Bucktails continued to drill and grumble, grumble and drill until the spring blossomed into early June. With every passing day, rumors raced on legs of their own from the Peninsula. News of the Union advance to within a few miles of Richmond and of a fierce battle at Fair Oaks on the last day of May set the riflemen to cleaning their muskets feverishly in anticipation of action.

Finally on June 8th, Captain Ed Irvin rushed beaming from headquarters to roust his Company K boys from their tents. Taps had sounded, and the Bucktails had just crawled into their blankets when he burst shouting into camp.

"Up an' at 'em," howled Irvin. "We got a little march ahead of us tonight."

"Did we get called up? Did we?" jabbered Zack Swift, scrambling from his tent to tug on his captain's coat sleeve like an excited schoolboy.

"What do you think? Get your gear packed. Let's go!"

Like a bear stung by bees, Keener scrambled pell-mell from his tent, almost ripping it in half. Jack Swift, meanwhile, hopped on one leg pulling on his trousers, while his brother Jude frantically stuffed gear into his haversack. Private Conklin was so flustered that he tripped over the stones of the still smoking fire pit and crashed to the ground amid a shower of sparks.

Only Sergeant Blett seemed unaffected by the news. Calmly, he took down his half of the dog tent he shared with Conklin and stowed it in his knapsack. The full moon made it easy for him to see, and he grinned at the bedlam around him.

"What's so dang amusin', Sergeant?" asked Jude, as he rushed to lend Zack a hand with his packing.

"You remind me of my little ones getting ready to visit their granny at Thanksgiving," laughed Daniel. "Only they're excited about all the food they'll be eating, while you fellas are hurrying to put yourselves in danger."

An hour passed before the Bucktails assembled on the road that led downriver. It was a pleasant, warm spring night. The troops marched effortlessly along gaping at the Virginia countryside bathed in bright moonlight. A chorus of frogs serenaded them as they walked. Several times startled owls fled on great, flapping wings. With the Rebels occupied elsewhere, there was no need for caution, and jokes passed up and down the ranks along with easy laughter.

The Bucktails marched all night. At the first glimmer of dawn, they heard the sound of busy hammers. When they tramped around a bend in the Rappahannock, they spotted a work crew of blue ants putting the finishing touches on a wharf. A navy transport was anchored in the river awaiting completion of this landing.

"Look at the smoke pourin' from that ship out yonder," gasped Jack Swift with alarm. "Do ya think the Reb navy hit it with a cannon round?"

"No, that's a steamer," chided Keener. "Don't ya see that there smokestack stickin' up out o' the deck? That means there's a steam engine powerin' her."

"How would you know," mocked Jude, "when the only thing you've ever seen floatin' was a raft made o' logs?"

"Yeah, if it's got an engine, how come there's masts with sails in the front an' back?" questioned Jack.

"Boy, you Swifts sure stick together," replied Joe. "I reckon ya won't be-lieve me 'til ya burns yer hand on the side o' that smokestack, so I might jess as well shut my trap."

"You boys better listen to Private Keener," said Captain Irvin, drawing a spyglass from his inside coat pocket. "Look. I can just make out our ship's name. She's the South America, by thunder!"

The wharf was finally finished while the Bucktails were eating breakfast, and their transport glided in to be moored there with strong rope. Zack and Jack gawked in wonderment at the sleek ship constructed of painted timber. Joe Keener and Enos Conklin even stopped chewing on their hardtack long enough to drink in the wide decks and the lifeboats hanging along the sides. Before anyone could comment on their impressions of the South America, the

13

squealing of bosuns' pipes and the badgering of officers were urging them into line and up the groaning gangplank. Zack and Jack gripped their muskets tightly and stepped with trepidation onto the transport. They had to be prodded forward by Sergeant Blett before they crossed the deck to the place assigned to the Bucktails near the fore railing. Jude Swift kept glancing at the belching smokestack protruding from the middle of the deck like it was a dragon thirsting for his blood. "Go over an' touch it," urged Keener when he saw the lad's anxiety. "Go on."

"No sir-ee, Joe. I'd rather stick my head down a cannon barrel."

The Rappahannock was calm and smooth when the Bucktails began their journey to the Peninsula. The air was balmy, which made even their deck passage pleasant. The ship was large enough not only to transport the riflemen, but all the rest of the First Brigade of the Pennsylvania Reserves, as well. Most of the soldiers had never been off dry land and sat rooted to the deck with blank expressions pasted on their faces.

Joe Keener was feeling a little sick, so he staggered off by himself in case he had to vomit. He was just getting used to the rolling of the ship when he felt someone's eyes boring through his back. Glancing over his shoulder, he found a vaguely familiar group of Berdan's Sharpshooters pointing at him and making threatening gestures. Several men's green coats sported deep tears, and one marksman's hat was smashed so flat that it was a wonder it sat on his head. Finally, Berdan's men crawled to their feet and swaggered to where Keener was perched along the railing.

"I didn't know they allowed circus bears aboard a U.S. vessel," growled a lanky, cold-eyed sergeant through badly scarred lips.

"You're wrong," snorted a green coated corporal with a recently broken nose. "This brute isn't smart enough to perform in a circus."

"Let's pitch him overboard and see if his trainer at least taught him to swim," shouted a private with a cauliflower ear.

"What seems to be the trouble, Private Keener?" asked Captain Irvin, rising to get between Joe and his assailants.

"I reckon these here fellas can't hit nothin' with them Sharps o' theirs, so they took ta shootin' off their mouths instead."

The squad of Berdan's Sharpshooters snarled under their breaths and inched closer at Keener's insult. Several soldiers bunched their fists menacingly before shoving them in their pockets. Only Captain Irvin's rank kept the men's anger from boiling over.

"It's clear that you fellows don't like each other very much," said the captain when Keener and the sharpshooters continued to glare at each other. "Instead of fighting it out and going to the brig, why don't we settle this another way?"

"What other way?" grunted the sergeant.

"What other way, sir!" corrected Irvin.

"What other way, sir?"

"We Bucktails will play you in a baseball game."

"Baseball? Why, yes! All the men in my squad are born hitters, and they'll beat you Bucktails' brains out. Some of them even played professionally. I can't wait to whip that big brute. . . er. . . private. . . in baseball, sir."

"When we get to the Peninsula then, Sergeant?"

"Yes, sir!"

CHAPTER THREE:
VOYAGE TO WAR

The <u>South America</u> steamed down the Rappahannock River, trailing black smoke. The day remained calm and beautiful. The Bucktails, having grown accustomed to the ship, lounged about enjoying the sunshine and the passing vistas.

"This sure beats marchin' all ta heck," sighed Enos Conklin, stretching his long legs on the deck.

"Yeah, there ain't no dust ta eat er gallinippers ta slap at here," chortled Joe. "I heared tell that in the swamps o' the Peninsula there's skeeters so big they kin drain a man o' his blood if he falls asleep without his blanket pulled over 'im."

"An' how 'bout them water moccasins?" added Jude Swift with a shudder.

"Them snakes is more aggressive than any timber rattler," replied Keener. "They'll swim fer ya an' won't quit bitin' 'til you're plumb dead. An' big! Why, some o' 'em is thick 'round as my leg."

"Jude, don't listen ta him," said Zack with a wide grin that contorted the long cut on his face. "He's full o' more hot air than one o' them observation balloons they use ta spy on the Rebs."

"That's right," seconded Sergeant Blett. "Keener's told so many yarns that he's starting to believe them himself. I just can't figure why he joined the army when he could make a lot more money as a manure spreader on some backwater farm."

"I's jess as much o' a patriot as you, sir," replied Keener with a hurt look. "Kin I help it I got dragged inta a bar fight up Curwensville way an' couldn't pay fer what I busted? I'm still sendin' that barkeep some o' my pay each month. I never knowed a mirror im-ported from New York City was so ex-pensive. Otherwise, I'da never bounced a fella's skull off it er got all that glass stuck in my hand."

"Now, that I can believe," grinned Jack Swift, "seein' ya got the scars ta prove it."

"An' you're jess as baby smooth as when ya left yer mama. Why in tarnation did a cub like you ever leave home ta tramp all over God's green earth?"

"Someone had ta take care o' Zack and Jude."

"Yeah, Joe, don't let his boyish looks fool ya none," said Zack. "You shoulda seen 'im bayonet them Rebs at Dranesville."

"An' here I thought he was too squeamish ta stick his fork in a roastin' goose ta see if it was done," guffawed Keener. "Come on. Why did you Swift boys en-list?"

"Our pap was a blacksmith," replied Jude, "an' he was as hard as the metal he forged."

"An' he sure tested our mettle every chance he got," winced Zack.

"Yeah, we weren't allowed ta make no mistakes," continued Jude, "er Pap's fist was sure ta find us. He weren't no easier on Ma, neither, so she finally lit out."

"That same week," mumbled Jack, "Pap flew inta a rage an' almost snapped Zack's eye out with a ridin' whip jess 'cause he was playin' instead o' workin'."

"None o' us was gonna stick 'round after that," croaked Zack, absently tracing the scar on his face. "We run off after dark as soon as the old man was asleep."

"Captain Irvin found us wanderin' 'round Curwensville kinda dazed like," added Jude. "He knew us 'cause we played baseball tagether fer the town team. He give us somethin' ta eat an' said if we was lookin' fer work we should join this here company he was startin'. We needed ta git out o' that neck o' the woods be-fore Pap caught up ta us, sure as shootin', so here we is marchin' an' fightin' an' makin' men o' ourselves."

Thoughtfully, Keener scratched his thick crop of red

17

hair. Afterward, he lit his pipe and said, "Come ta think o' it, the fella I smashed inta that mirror was a blacksmith. He was the one picked a fight with me. He was mighty ornery 'til I mopped up the tavern with 'im. I sure hope it was yer pa, 'cause that fella weren't gonna whoop no younguns fer some time after I tied 'im inta a pretzel!"

"What 'bout you, Sergeant Blett?" asked Zack after favoring Keener with an appreciative grin. "You seem like too smart a fella ta have joined us yokels. Why did you decide ta en-list?"

"I was a carriage maker but liked playing soldier in the militia group I captained better. I guess I wanted to be part of some great adventure."

"Ah, don't let 'im fool ya," brayed Keener. "He jess wanted ta es-cape a naggin' wife like every other married fella in Mr. Lincoln's army!"

"At least my wife only chides me at night," laughed Blett. "Your woman, Madam Whiskey, gives you a hard time well into the afternoon of the next day."

The Bucktails continued to banter back and forth until the sun began to sink into the western end of the river behind them. Just before dark, the South America hove to in a deep channel near the north bank and dropped anchor. There was no extra food aboard to feed the troops, so Daniel Blett's squad gnawed down a quick dinner of dry hardtack and then fell asleep on the gently rocking deck. Captain Irvin, however, did not sleep at all. With Berdan's Sharpshooters prowling about in the shadows, he was careful not to let Private Keener out of his sight until the ship's engines sputtered into life at dawn.

The South America steamed down the Rappahannock for two more hours until it reached the jagged headland marking Chesapeake Bay. Here, the wind picked up dramatically, and the Bucktails grabbed for their hats before they were swept off into the foaming water. The riflemen were also treated to the sight of a vast flock of seagulls circling white in the cloudless sky. Several curious birds dove from great heights to have a better look at the steamer.

18

Squawking their high pierced shrieks, they glided effortlessly past causing Keener to remark, "If them birds is comin' down fer a free meal, they's outta luck. I'd throw 'em some hardtack, but if they ate it, they crash inta the sea, sure as shootin'."

"Why's that?" asked Jack.

"'Cause them sheet iron crackers would weigh 'em down so much, they'd be too dang heavy ta fly."

Out in Chesapeake Bay, the steam transport was buffeted by waves that sent the Bucktails scrambling for the railings. The South America pitched and rolled until everyone but Sergeant Blett was puking over the side.

"Joe, your face is greener than Berdan's sack coat," needled Daniel.

"Don't say that," groaned Keener, "er I'll be sick an' mad, too."

"Heck, you're never sick o' bein' mad," said Zack between retches, "so what's the diff'rence?"

Exhausted from their vomiting, the Bucktails slumped over the rails until Blett shouted, "Look, fellas, there's the mouth of a river and Yorktown beside it dead ahead."

"How do ya know that, Sergeant, when ya ain't been out o' yer own carriage house 'til the start o' this here war?" grunted Jude. "You wouldn't know Yorktown if ya read the town sign."

"Just look at the fort there. It's the same one that's in all the history books. That's where Washington whipped the British and won our freedom."

"Yeah, an' now we's back ta force the Rebs inta the Union. Seems kinda funny, don't it?" sighed Conklin, his face white beneath his dirty stubble of beard.

Churning into the York River, the South America entered less turbulent waters, and the Bucktails returned to lounging on the deck. The York estuary was not half as wide as that of the Rappahannock. The banks were overgrown with thick trees, and Jude Swift kept peering nervously toward shore until Sergeant Blett asked, "What's ailing you, lad?"

"Don't them thick growed oaks over yonder look like a perfect place fer snipers? Maybe we should send a lookout up the mast."

"Johnny Reb's too busy defending Richmond to pay attention to us," assured Daniel. "You better relax while you still can."

"Yeah, you're fidgety as a coon treed in a low saplin'," chortled Keener. "If ya didn't have yer brothers' face, I'd swear you weren't part o' the Swift clan. They's always waggin' their tails like beagle pups, while you mope 'round like a sad, old bloodhound."

"He's got plenty o' reason ta be sad with the dangers we's about ta face," said Enos. "I sometimes wish I'd never left off millin' grain ta join up with you fellas."

"Hey, the mill will still be there when ya git back. I'd rather grind up the Reb army myself," chuckled Zack.

"That's jess like you, all right," needled Jack. "You was the one who always busted the few toys we got."

"My children are destructive imps, too," sighed Blett. "I hope their poor mother can keep their daily rebellion in check until we put down the one we're neck-deep in."

The Bucktails grew suddenly silent when their transport slowed its engines and entered a small, winding river. The woods grew even thicker here, and shadows crept to the very water's edge. "This is the Pamunkey," muttered Sergeant Blett. "I saw it on a map back in Falmouth."

"It's a good thing we don't de-pend on Joe fer inferma-tion," joked Zack. "The only thing he's ever studied is the bottom o' an ale tankard."

"At least I's old enough ta drink ale," replied Keener testily. "You Swifts is still suckin' on pabulum."

The <u>South America</u> blew three mighty blasts from its steam whistle. Blett's squad stared over the rail to see a bustling village appear through an opening in the trees on the south bank of the Pamunkey. Another steamer was moored at the far end of the wharf ahead. A horde of blue coats struggled to unload supplies from this heavy laden vessel. Wooden boxes full of food and ammunition were manhandled down the gangplank and into waiting wagons. Full wagons, in turn, creaked down a muddy street to a row of boxcars drawn up behind a smoking locomotive. A bold sign nailed on the side of the train depot proclaimed, "White House."

There was a great grinding as the Bucktails' transport shut down its engines to glide alongside the wharf. Sailors in baggy, blue uniforms scurried like monkeys to secure the vessel with ropes thicker than a man's arm. The <u>South America</u> had no sooner docked when the troops were ordered to line up and disembark.

Sergeant Blett's squad wobbled down the gangplank and onto the wooden dock vibrating with countless feet. There they merged with a sea of Bucktails who milled about aimlessly until Major Stone moved from company to company barking out commands. Soon, the regiment untangled itself and slogged along a muddy street past Union headquarters.

"Do you know who lived in that place before Little Mac took it over?" asked Daniel, pointing toward the comfortable, old home.

"No, who?" asked Jack with a wide-eyed stare.

"That's the house Bobby Lee grew up in. His son was still living there before the Union invasion."

"They shoulda burned the dang place ta the ground, then," muttered Keener.

"And ruin all that history?" gasped Blett in disbelief.

"Hey, it's hot e-nough already here without startin' no fire," added Enos Conklin, mopping his forehead with a stained handkerchief.

"Hell's supposed ta be scaldin'," replied Joe. "Ya better gits used ta it."

As the Bucktails reached a whitewashed shop near the outskirts of town, they encountered a gaunt man holding a sign that read, "For the Embalming of the Dead." Nearby, two undertakers dressed in freshly pressed black suits stood on the street passing out leaflets that detailed their services.

"I'll take one o' them papers," guffawed Keener to the

nearest embalmer, "if ya promise ta git started right away. A fella can't be too pre-pared fer war, ya know."

"Yeah, but ya gots ta promise it won't ruin our a-bility ta chaw on hardtack," chortled Zack Swift.

"Er ruin how handsome we is," laughed Jack.

"But first, I'd like ta see what ya kin do with the major's horse," smirked Keener, pointing ahead to the scrawny gelding Roy Stone guided up the street.

The Bucktails gave the undertakers a mock salute and then continued to march to an open field just beyond White House where a makeshift camp sprouted from the ground as if by magic. Soon, the riflemen were erecting their own doghouses and starting fires to boil coffee. As they gathered around their fire pits to socialize, two wagons piled high with rations came sloshing up the road toward them. A ragged cheer rose from the camp, followed by the riflemen's mad dash to refill their long empty haversacks.

The quartermaster corps issued the Bucktails salted beef and two days' supply of hardtack. When the ravenous soldiers again sat down to have dinner, they had only gobbled a few bites of their new rations before Enos Conklin muttered, "Look at this here pickled mule them rascals give us. It's so green, it looks like somethin' growed on a tree."

"An' this teeth-duller's so wormy, it's not fit fer turkey buzzards," cried Jude Swift, pitching his hardtack on the ground.

"Hey, don't throw that here," ordered Sergeant Blett, "or our camp will be crawling with vermin. I don't know about you, but I'd rather take on the whole Reb army by myself than have a river rat crawl over my face when I laid down to sleep."

"Yeah, pitch yer hardtack over yonder by Berdan's camp," suggested Joe. "Them fellas wouldn't mind a night visit from their kin."

Jude gathered up a haversack load of wormy hardtack from his squad and trudged back to the road to chuck it in a ditch. When he returned, the Bucktails were busy cooking rancid beef that stunk so badly it killed his hunger. The others burned the meat black before forcing it down their gullets.

Halfway through the meal, Daniel Blett noticed several pieces of hardtack thrown near his feet. After growling a rare curse, he said, "I thought I asked you boys not to chuck those teeth-dullers around camp. Are those yours, Joe?"

Keener, who was seated next to Dan, flashed a mischievous grin. "They ain't mine, Sergeant," he replied. "I reckon the weevils in them hard biscuits got lonesome lyin' in that ditch over yonder an' de-cided ta crawl back here fer some good Bucktail fellership."

"Well, then you better pitch that hardtack in the river and drown those weevils," muttered Blett. "Otherwise, you'll be pulling rat patrol all night just outside my dog tent."

The Swift brothers could have used what they learned about blacksmithing in the Union Army, for most units carried anvils and portable forges with them. Also, they could have enlisted as farriers and done horseshoeing for the cavalry. Above, smithy reenactor, Dennis Murray, and his assistants shape molten metal on a portable anvil.

CHAPTER FOUR:
BUCKTAIL BASEBRAWL

After roll call the next morning, a squad of haughty Berdan's Sharpshooters swaggered through the Bucktails' camp to Captain Irvin's tent. Ed Irvin sat outside in a canvas chair filling out a report. He nodded to the green uniformed soldiers as they snapped to attention before him. Saluting arrogantly, the Berdan sergeant barked, "If it pleases the captain, I wish to remind him of the baseball game he promised our regiment. It would be best played today before we move upriver."

"At ease, men. It does please me to remember our game. Why don't you go lay out the field on the White House parade grounds while I get my team together."

"What rules do you play by, Captain? We favor those used by the Knickerbocker Baseball Club of New York City."

"I doubt if General Doubleday, who invented the game, even heard of those," laughed Ed. "Why don't we just play town ball?"

"Town ball?" muttered the sergeant, stiffening.

"Sure. You hit the ball and run around the bases to home. If you can't get all the way home, you're only safe if you stay on first, second, or third base. You're dead if you're hit with a batted or thrown ball or your fly ball is caught in the air or on one bounce. A striker who swings at and misses three pitches in a row is also dead. After three strikers are declared dead, the other club bats. The first club to reach one hundred tallies is the winner. Are these rules satisfactory?"

"That's not as formal as the ball we're used to," grumbled the sergeant, "but we agree. What stakes shall we play for? How about a greenback per man?"

"How about the pride of our regiments!" snapped Irvin. "That should be enough to motivate any soldier, regular or reserve."

"Yes, sir! We'll see you at the parade grounds."

After the U.S. Sharpshooters had marched stiffly from camp, Ed ducked inside his tent and fetched two hand carved bats he used in his hometown league. With a sudden grin he thought, I'm sure glad I brought my lumber along. I heard baseball was the Union Army's favorite game, and I've been itching to have a crack at another outfit. Before the war, our club nine won the Curwensville championship two summers in a row. And, boy, can the Swift brothers ever play the field! Zack, Jack, and Jude may not be professionals like the puffed up Berdan dandies, but they sure give us Bucktails more than a fighting chance.

With his bats thrown over his shoulder, the captain strolled toward a breakfast campfire where Sergeant Blett's squad was still grumbling about the poor rations issued them the day before. When Zack saw what Irvin was carrying, he leaped up and shouted, "God bless you, Captain. Just what we need to raise our spirits. Baseball!"

"Against Berdan's men, to boot," beamed Irvin. "Up and at 'em."

"With as fast as you Swift boys can fly, we got this game in the bag!" yelped Enos Conklin. "Just slap the ball inta the outfield an' score, score, score!"

"Yeah, we'll run them right off the field," chuckled Sergeant Blett.

"An' if a couple o' them Berdan yahoos gits runned over on the baselines, all the better," chortled Joe.

By the time the Bucktails arrived at the parade grounds, the Berdan club had laid out the playing field. Wooden stakes protruding four feet from the ground served as the bases, while a hardtack box was used for the plate. A ditch full of stagnant water formed the right field boundary. A hickory grove provided the homerun fence. The field itself was flatten into a smooth surface by countless drilling troops that had bivouacked at White House on their way to war up the Peninsula.

Ed Irvin stuffed a wad of tobacco in his mouth and stared out at the opposing nine that already had assumed their defensive positions. A barrel-chested giant stood solid as a stone gate near first base. Second and shortstop were manned by able hands that gobbled up every grounder hit to them by the corporal whose nose Keener had busted. Joe's nemesis, the cold-eyed sergeant, rounded out the basetenders. He played third with a professional flair that made Captain Irvin swallow his Adam's apple several times before checking out the speedy, practiced scouts who roamed the outfield shagging flies.

The behind, though, was by far the most fearsome of the Berdan nine. He had massive arms and legs and was built low to the ground like a hickory stump. A scowl settled on a mug scarred by many encounters with sliding base runners and balls fouled off his chin and forehead. He answered to "McKee" whenever the corporal asked him to fetch a ball that got away from him.

"Look at that fella," whistled Jack, pointing to the Berdan catcher.

"He's perfect fer the be-hind position all right," chortled Keener, "'cause he looks jess like the rear end o' an army mule!"

"You fellows can bat first," called the sergeant from third base when Irvin's club had filed onto the field. "You're the visitors, and you're going to need all the chances to bat you can get to beat us!"

Ed Irvin glared defiantly at the sergeant. Then he told his players to huddle up as he announced the batting order and told the boys where to play in the field. Jude Swift was chosen to hit first, and he took the lighter of the two bats his captain offered him. "I remember this beauty," he said with a confident smile. "I went four fer four with her in the champeenship game last August."

"That lumber ain't gonna do ya no good," snarled

27

McKee. "We're gonna massacre ya. Jess wait an' see. Wait an' see!"

Swift stepped up to take his knocks. Pounding the bat on the ground, he growled, "The only thing you's gonna see, fella, is me strikin' the ball clean over yer outfield scouts."

While Jude and McKee glared at each other, the Berdan corporal paced off the thrower's position forty-five feet from home base and drew a line in the dirt with his brogan. Afterward, he turned, crossed his legs, and presented the ball. Before Jude was ready, the hurler took a quick step forward and flung the ball underhand with all his might at Swift's head. Jude jerked back at the last instant, and the eight-inch, leather wrapped sphere whizzed within a quarter of an inch of the lad's nose.

"Look alive, ducktail," growled the behind, McKee. "That was the slowest pitch you's gonna get."

"Hey, you have to toss the ball where the striker wants it!" shouted Captain Irvin. "That's in the rules!"

"Sorry," replied the thrower with a smirk. "The ball must have slipped out of my hand."

"Yeah, right!" growled Keener. "Jess like my hands is gonna slip 'round yer throat if ya don't play fair."

A determined look settled on Swift's face. He stepped back up to the plate and swung with all his might at the next pitch. The ball caromed off the end of the bat to the hurler. Before Jude took two steps toward first base, he got drilled square in the ribs by a thrown ball. The air whistled from his lungs, and he crumbled into a limp heap.

"You're dead!" yelled the obnoxious sergeant from third base. "Next striker."

After Daniel Blett and Jack Swift dragged Jude from the baseline, Zack stepped up to home base. The Berdan corporal fired his first pitch behind Zack's head to unnerve him. The tactic didn't work because Swift drilled the second pitch up the middle, just missing the hurler's right ear. Then, Zack sprinted for all he was worth as the ball squirted past a diving outfielder and rolled and rolled. With the cheers of his club nine ringing in his ears, the lad rounded the bases to tally the Bucktail's first ace.

Zack's hit sparked a first inning rally that saw his team bat around twice before the final out was recorded. With glares and growls, Berdan's men strode from the field, while the Bucktails jubilantly trooped from the sidelines to take up their defensive positions. Ed Irvin was the thrower. Joe Keener was at first, Jack at second, Zack at short, and Daniel at third. The scouts in the outfield were all lean, agile youngsters who had played town ball with Irvin. The behind was Jude Swift. He had only had the wind knocked out of him and was now simmering mad.

The obnoxious corporal was the first Berdan striker. He pounded the plate with the thick club he used for a bat, shooting a cloud of dust into the squatting Jude's eyes. After he spit tobacco juice on the behind's shoe, he glared hatefully at Irvin and blared, "Toss it in here, Captain. I played in New York City. Now, you're gonna see how a professional plays this game."

"If ya keeps spittin' that tobaccy," growled Jude, "ya ain't gonna see nothin' but my fist!"

"Ah, go chase yourself!" snarled the corporal, again stepping up to bat.

"Same ta you, fella!"

The corporal swung through Irvin's first pitch before drilling a grounder in the hole between short and third. Zack Swift dodged deftly to his right and blocked the ball with his shins. Before the ball could squirt away, he snatched it up and fired it toward the streaking corporal. The ball clocked the runner in the shoulder two steps from first base, and he yelped with pain as Irvin declared him dead.

"What kind of play was that?" groused the corporal as he headed back to the sidelines, rubbing his new bruise. "A real player woulda caught the ball instead of blockin' it."

"An' a real pro-fessional from New York woulda ducked," chortled Keener.

The next two strikers also made the mistake of driving the ball to Zack. Each time, the nimble youngster knocked down smoking liners and then struck the streaking base runners before they arrived at first.

"Zack, how in tarnation did you lead them fellas like that?" asked Joe when the Bucktails had charged from the field for their second chance to bat.

"Jess like shootin' a runnin' buck," grinned Swift. "Instead o' peddlin' lead, I fires the ball."

Down fifteen to nothing after one inning had the Berdan nine boiling. Flushed cheeks, bristling beards, and exaggerated movements were tell-tale signs of the basetenders' frustration. The hurler now took to windmilling the ball for added velocity. It made no difference, for Zack smashed the first pitch he saw far over the centerfield scout's head. With a whoop, he sprinted for first, waving his Bucktail hat over his head like a banner. As he rounded the base, the barrel-chested giant lurking there stuck out his foot and sent Swift sprawling on his face. In an instant Zack was up and scrambling for second. There, the basetender grabbed him by the coat sleeve until he ripped free. Between second and third the shortstop tried pushing the runner to the ground. Swift dodged him and made for the cold-eyed Berdan sergeant who cuffed Zack in the face, again sending him crashing to the field. By then, the ball had been retrieved by an outfield scout who heaved it back to third base. The sergeant snagged the ball out of the air and turned to whip it at Zack where he lay writhing.

"You're dead!" bellowed the sergeant, when the ball smashed Swift in the middle of the back. "Next striker."

Grabbing the heaviest club he could find, Joe Keener stepped up to the plate. "What kinda dang game is this?" he growled. "Wrestlin' er baseball? If ya wanna play rough, you jess brung it ta the right fella!"

Keener creamed the first pitch the corporal hurled and then lowered his head as he charged toward first. The ball was hit so hard to the second baseman that he couldn't dodge to defend himself. It struck him square in the face, sending up a shower of blood and knocking him senseless. While the shortstop retrieved the ball, Joe smashed into the hulking first baseman and drove him into the infield turf. The thud of the collision barely faded away when the two players were flailing away at each other with their ham-sized fists.

In an instant, the Bucktails rushed onto the field to aid Keener. Zack Swift charged the opposing shortstop and tackled him to the ground. Jude, meanwhile, cut the legs out from under the attacking hurler. Even Daniel Blett lost his temper, engaging in a spirited boxing match with the cold-eyed snake of a sergeant. He hit the Berdan ringleader with a flurry of punches that came so fast and furious that the man spent more time covering up than fighting back. Jack, too, was really angry. He leaped on the back of the burly McKee and rode him like an unbroken stallion. The behind bucked and snorted, but no matter how hard he tried, he couldn't dislodge the youngest Swift brother.

The sounds of the pitched battle woke Major Stone dozing at headquarters. Jerking awake, he ran his hand through his full black beard as he listened intently to the skirmish. Finally, he bellowed, "Adjutant Hartshorne! Go see what's causing that ruckus. It can't be the Rebs, or there'd be plenty of musket fire by now."

"Yes, sir," replied the adjutant solemnly. "I'll bet our boys are at it again. Black eyes and split lips are as much the badge of this outfit as the buck tail is."

"Amen to that, Ross."

Ross Hartshorne saluted Major Stone and jammed his kepi cap over the concerned creases on his forehead. Outside, he leaped on his mount and galloped off toward the distant melee. "What we need is for the spring campaign to begin," he muttered. "That's about all that will keep our darn boys from killing each other."

Hartshorne arrived at the parade grounds in a whirlwind of dust and curses. Keener and the giant first baseman were still wrestling for all they were worth, and the incensed Jude was trouncing the Berdan corporal. Jack, too, was still clinging desperately to McKee as Daniel Blett delivered a knockout blow to the other sergeant.

Ed Irvin stood laughing on the sidelines until he caught sight of the adjutant galloping toward him. With difficulty, he composed himself and yelled above the din, "Company K, attention!"

"You heard the captain!" blared Hartshorne like an out-of-tune bugle. "Fall into rank! Berdan's company! Into rank!"

The adjutant fired his pistol twice in the air before his commands were answered. Only then, did the battered men crawl to their feet and straggle sheepishly into line.

"What's going on here, Captain Irvin?" demanded Hartshorne when order had been restored.

"Before transferring to the Signal Corps, you were one of us Curwensville boys," replied Ed. "Don't you remember, Ross, what fighting wildcats we have in this company? We were just playing ourselves a friendly game of baseball."

"Basebrawl, you mean!" growled the adjutant, his dark moustache flaring. "If you haven't heard, General McClellan is coming to review our regiment day after tomorrow. I want all of you to return to camp and spit polish those buckles and boots. And wash those uniforms! You will either make a good impression on the general, or you'll be walking guard duty with knapsacks full of rocks until you can't walk it anymore. Dismissed!"

When the adjutant had turned his horse and rode furiously away, Zack Swift said with a smirk to Blett, "I'm sure glad them Berdan boys agreed ta use our town ball rules, Sergeant."

"Why's that?"

"'Cause if we played like they do in New York City, I reckon weapons would find their way inta the next con-test. Don't ya think we oughta go shake hands with them fellas now that we beat the tar out o' them?"

"Yes," said Captain Irvin, overhearing Zack's remark. "I agree with the private. It's time we display good sportsmanship and save the rest of our aggression for the Rebs."

"An' fer Major Stone's toady--that stinkin' Hartshorne," whispered Keener.

"Ah, Ross isn't so bad," assured Sergeant Blett. "He's just ambitious. Ever since he was a wee lad, he wanted to be a general."

"Until then I reckon he'll settle fer bein' a general pain," chuckled Zack before reaching to shake hands with the still grumbling Berdan sharpshooter he had just pummeled.

Bucktail reenactor Waylon Walck takes his hacks during a baseball game at the St. Marys Middle School Civil War Days held in St. Marys, PA, during May of 2004.

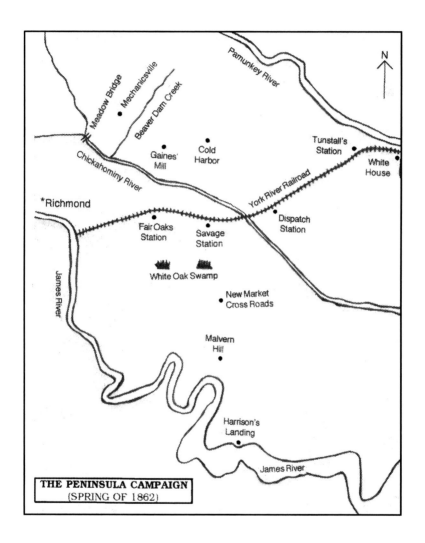

N

Pamunkey River

Meadow Bridge

Mechanicsville

Beaver Dam Creek

Tunstall's
Station

White
House

Gaines'
Mill

Cold
Harbor

Chickahominy River

York River Railroad

*Richmond

Dispatch
Station

Fair Oaks
Station

Savage
Station

White Oak Swamp

James River

New Market
Cross Roads

Malvern
Hill

Harrison's
Landing

James River

THE PENINSULA CAMPAIGN
(SPRING OF 1862)

CHAPTER FIVE:
THE CAMPAIGN BEGINS

Hampered by the bumps and bruises received in their baseball game, the Bucktails broke camp the next morning and limped up the Peninsula toward Richmond. They followed the York River Railroad that provided solid ground for their march. As Joe Keener hobbled along, he noted the heavily timbered swamp to either side of the railroad grade.

"Heck o' a place fer a fight," concluded Keener, nodding to Sergeant Blett.

"Lots of cover, anyway," replied Daniel.

"Yeah, fer Reb snipers," grunted Enos Conklin.

The Bucktails' march continued until late afternoon. Often, they were forced to leave the grade while heavily loaded trains rattled past on the way to supply General McClellan's troops entrenched east of the Rebel capital. The first time a smoke-spewing locomotive appeared, Jack waved wildly until the engineer blew his whistle in reply.

"By jiminy, ain't that engine grand!" exclaimed the youngest Swift.

"Ya ain't foolin' me none," laughed Zack. "All yer praise o' that engine is jess ta throw us off. With the way you eats, you're only thinkin' 'bout the pro-visions stacked in them boxcars."

"One thing's fer dang sure," replied Jack. "We wouldn't have ta worry none 'bout starvin' if we pulled guard duty on this here line. Talk 'bout a soft job."

The Bucktails trudged past Tunstall's Station to Dispatch Station before orders were finally given for them to fall out. Sore and exhausted, they stumbled off into a woodlot to set up camp. From the ever-present swamplands croaking frogs and the eerie calls of night birds worried them as they set up their dog tents. Soon they had low fires burning to cook the rest of their rancid meat ration that Jack wolfed down despite its foul stench.

"Jack, you must have the gullet o' a dang mongrel pup ta di-gest that salt horse," muttered Keener, pitching his own meat into the fire.

"Hey, don't waste that!" protested the lad. "If ya got any more, give it here!"

Just before dark, one last train rumbled up the nearby track and braked noisily to a stop. The door of a boxcar creaked open and several wooden crates and canvas sacks were hastily unloaded into the charge of Lieutenant Patton, the regiment's quartermaster. While the locomotive again lurched into motion, fresh rations and a load of mail were distributed to the suddenly revived Bucktails.

"Lookee here," sighed Enos contentedly after chomping on a hardtack biscuit. "These teeth-dullers must be fresh 'cause I ain't bit through one weevil."

"Even better!" whooped Joe. "I got me a letter from my old pal, Hosea Curtis."

"Well, don't jess set there grinnin' like ya shot a twelve point buck," chortled Zack. "Read it ta us."

"Yeah, I'd like ta know how many taverns he busted up over yonder in the Shenandoah," Jude said wryly.

"Er how many barrels o' forty-rod he emptied by hisself," laughed Zack.

"Kane's boys woulda been too busy marchin' an' fightin' fer Hosea ta pull any o' them shenanigans," replied Joe. "He might love a ripsnortin' good time, but I never knowed him ta miss a day's work 'cause o' it."

"That's unless Curtis was in the custody of some sheriff," winked Blett.

"Come on. Read the letter, will ya?" urged Jack, inching closer so he wouldn't miss a word.

"Yeah, read it be-fore Jack throws hisself a tantrum," kidded Zack.

"Okay. Here goes:

Howdy Joe,

Us boys just marched the entire length of the Shenandoah Valley, and I figgered you might like to know how we done. Colonel Kane was right about us outperformin' the cavalry. We was still fightin' long after every critter company's horseshoes wore out, and they plumb had to quit.

Yes, sir, we kept right on that rascal Stonewall Jackson's heels 'til we got bushwhacked at Harrisonburg. There we dusted that Reb general, Turner Ashby, we did. We was told not to shoot any man on a horse 'cause he'd be an officer and a gentleman. So first, we killed Ashby's mount and then the general hisself. There was too gol-dang many Rebs in the end, though, and we was forced to retreat. Kane got wounded and captured. Then Captain Taylor and the Jewett lad from my squad went out lookin' fer the colonel. They got picked up too. Bucky Culp, the other lad I been wet-nursin', done got promoted to corporal for luggin' a wounded drummer from the field. I'd never tell Culp this, but I'm gol-dang proud of him. Hope to tip a few with you soon.

Your pal,
Hosea"

"So Stonewall Jackson escaped," said Daniel with a low whistle. "I'll bet he's heading here."

"Along with every other able-bodied Southern boy," added Enos. "You kin bet them Rebs will throw everything they got at us ta keep us from takin' Richmond."

"An' now that Bobbie Lee is leadin' 'em," shuddered Jude, "we best be pre-pared fer anything!"

The Bucktails continued to discuss the news received from Curtis until Captain Irvin rushed to their campsite and barked, "Okay, men, up and at 'em. Word's come that Johnny Reb cut the railroad behind us. Our brigade is to push the Rebs out of there and keep our supply lines open."

With excited yelps, the riflemen leaped to gather their gear. Once armed, they scurried to join General Reynolds'

First Brigade assembling into battle formation. With the six companies of Bucktails thrown forward as skirmishers, the Union force swept back down the railroad grade toward White House.

"Good thing the moon's shinin' so bright," whispered Jack as he slunk along through the woods bordering the railroad.

"Hope we spots the Rebs before they sees us," said Jude, dodging stealthily from tree to tree.

"Hey, Jack! Jude! Don't stray too far from the grade," hissed Captain Irvin. "You sure don't want to fall into the swamp."

"Yeah! That wouldn't be too <u>swift</u>," chortled Joe.

The Bucktails continued to inch along the margins of the railroad grade until flames burst suddenly from the horizon ahead. Keeping to the shadows, the riflemen rushed toward a distant station illuminated by a long row of blazing boxcars. Sporadic shots resonated up the tracks along with the hair-raising howl of jubilant Rebels.

The First Rifles charged hard until they reached a section of track uprooted by the enemy. Here, Captain Irvin warned, "Slow down, Bucktails. Stay alert now."

"Listen to the captain," urged Blett. "Keep your eyes peeled for an ambush."

Cocking their Springfields, the Bucktails again crept forward toward the station. Between the moonlight and the fiercely burning cars, every detail of the train yard was brightly illuminated. Inching along, Joe Keener stepped over the dead bodies of two civilian workers. The smell of burning corn was in his nostrils, along with the reek of creosote from smoldering railroad ties. He observed downed telegraph poles and the cut lines dangling uselessly from those that still stood. He heard a groan emitting from the Tunstall station house and slipped inside to investigate.

A Yankee guard lay on the floor in a widening pool of blood. He had a belly wound, and his every breath caused him to wince with pain.

"What happened here?" asked Joe, bending to offer the

wounded man a hit from the whiskey flask he kept in his coat pocket.

"It was. . . Stuart. . . that. . . hit us," whimpered the guard.

"J.E.B.?"

"Yeah. . . We didn't. . . have a chance."

"Easy now. Easy!"

"He captured my whole outfit. . . and horses and mules. Burned boxcars. . . full of supplies. The scoundrel. . . shot me. . ."

A low sigh leaked from the soldier's lips before his body went limp. Jack Swift had followed Joe into the station, and Keener said to him, "What do ya think o' guardin' the railroad line now, laddie? Ain't such a soft job, after all."

"I wonder what Stuart's doin' in these parts? I sure wouldn't wanna meet up with him on the way back up the grade," gulped Jack.

"Probably out scoutin'. Once he knows the weak point in the Union line, he'll re-turn ta Richmond an' tell Bobbie Lee. Then our fat'll be fried!"

From outside, Keener heard Captain Irvin shout, "Douse those flames, boys. Hurry up before they spread to the station."

"Let's skedaddle," said Joe. "We best git out there an' help."

"What about him?" asked Jack, pointing to the dead soldier.

"Nothin' we kin do," muttered Keener, "'cept add 'im ta the butcher's bill."

The Bucktails formed a bucket brigade from a nearby swamp to the train yard and toiled for two hours before the flames engulfing the burning boxcars and wagons were extinguished. When they had finished their hot work, they marched numbly back down the tracks to their bivouac. The moon had disappeared behind thickening clouds, casting a pall of doom over the weary regiment.

The men were too tired to bellyache about their first

day of the new campaign. They crawled into their dog tents and slept without moving until bugles roused them at dawn. This time they were rousted out of their quarters to parade for General McClellan. After thoroughly scrubbing their weapons, uniforms, and themselves all morning, the general did not show up at eleven a.m. to review the troops.

"The problem is they held this here in-spection too early," groused Conklin as the men broke rank and filed dejectedly back to camp.

"Too early?" echoed Jack.

"Yeah, 'cause there ain't no general in the whole dang Union army that crawls outta his feather bed 'til noon."

CHAPTER SIX:
MECHANICSVILLE

The swamp was alive with the clamor of croaking frogs when the Bucktails set off again the next morning. Leaving the railroad grade, they slogged along a muddy road that paralleled the Chickahominy River. As the soldiers marched steadily toward the Union front lines, Keener studied the river basin below him. The terrain was thickly wooded and dotted with stagnant, marshy pools. Through an opening in the trees, he saw that the river itself often broke into several channels. Joe figured that even if the muddy water rose a little, the whole place would become an impassable bog. It looked to be about a mile from the highland where he walked to the highland that bordered the southern side of the Chickahominy Valley.

"If I was a general, I sure wouldn't want this here river dividin' my army," Joe said to Sergeant Blett, pointing below.

"Well, I heard that Little Mac's attack force is spread out to the south. Us boys are only on this side of the river to protect the Union supply base at White House. If we don't hold, communications will be cut. That means the rest of the army won't get hardtack or bullets and will be forced to retreat."

"It's bully to be given such responsibility," said Captain Irvin, overhearing their conversation. "I for one am proud to be assigned to General McCall's division."

"Yes, sir!" agreed the three Swift brothers, bursting into a ragged cheer.

The Bucktails tramped along until they heard the fevered sound of shovels gouging at the earth. Coming to a little rise, they saw just below them a horde of blue-coated infantry digging rifle pits on the eastern bank of a feeder stream. Keener judged the stream to be about six feet wide and plenty deep. The banks on either side were steep and would give attacking troops all kinds of fits. The stream flowed downhill until it joined the Chickahominy at a right angle.

Just as the First Rifles arrived at the entrenchment, a colonel galloped up the slope toward Major Stone. "Take your men to the extreme right flank and dig in," the officer ordered. "We must keep the Rebels from learning our strength, Major, so drumming and the firing of rifles is prohibited until our position is secure."

"Yes, sir," answered Stone. "Let's go, Bucktails. Get down there and get at it!"

The Bucktails toiled all afternoon hacking individual trenches in the loamy soil. Each trench was just the size of a soldier's body, so he could lie in a prone firing position. A mound of earth was piled in front of the rifle pit to stop Reb bullets from hitting the defender.

Fires were prohibited for security reasons. For supper the riflemen munched on the last of the hardtack they were given the day before. "I wonder how long it's been since any o' us fellas has had a fit meal?" wondered Enos when his stomach still growled after his rations were devoured.

"It had to have been at Falmouth," replied Sergeant Blett.

"That was three weeks ago," muttered Jude.

"The only reason we ate good there," reminded Joe, "is 'cause we got paid reg'lar an' could buy food an' corn squeezin's from the farmers."

"I kin still taste them strawberry pies I bought," sighed Jack with a dreamy, wide-eyed look.

"Yeah, gettin' caught with pie on yer face was a good thing at Falmouth," chortled Zack.

The Bucktails spent a damp night huddled in their rifle pits. At daybreak, as they stretched their cramped legs, orders arrived for them and the Fifth Regiment to go search

43

for the Confederates. Immediately, the riflemen scrambled from their trenches, forded Beaver Dam Creek, spread in a skirmish line, and slipped off to the west.

The First Rifles cut across country and then crept cautiously through a sleepy village named Mechanicsville. Joe thought the town was deserted until he heard the furtive scuffling of feet inside the whitewashed church they passed. Farther down the street a baby's cry was cut off in mid-wail. Then a little boy's demand to go outside to play was muffled by hidden hands.

The countryside remained eerily quiet until the reconnaissance force reached a sign reading "Meadow Bridge" about a mile west of Mechanicsville. "This is where General McCall said to wait," said Major Stone, running his hand through his black beard. "The Rebs are expected to cross here, and we're to hit them with everything we got!"

The words were barely out of Stone's mouth when a barrage of small arms fire exploded from the distance. "That must be the Illinois cavalry I was told to watch for. Companies B, D, and K, form up! Let's see if we can rescue those boys. The rest of you stay here and guard this bridge!" snapped the major.

Major Stone advanced the three Bucktail companies for a half-hour until they reached a place where three roads met. Digging a map from his saddle bag, Stone studied it for a moment and then bellowed, "Captain Wister, you remain here with Company B. Captain Jewett, proceed with Company D up that road to Atley's Station. The other road leads to, let's see, um. . . Crenshaw's Bridge. Captain Irvin, take Company K in that direction. One of you is bound to find our lost cavalry."

Ed Irvin ordered his men into battle formation, and they slunk one cautious step at a time toward Crenshaw's Bridge. Joe Keener glanced worriedly about him at the dense swamps that hemmed them in on either side of the narrow dirt lane. Finally, he muttered to Daniel Blett, "I reckon we's up a stump this time. If we smacks inta the whole Reb army, our only escape will be back down this here turkey track."

"That is if they don't unlimber a cannon and rake us with grapeshot."

"You boys worry too much," grinned Zack. "When we finds the Rebs, we'll pick 'em off like pigeons be-fore they git that cannon trained on us. After all, we's the best sharpshooters in this er any other dang army."

Company K continued to creep down the lane until they heard a sudden eruption of musket fire behind them. This was followed moments later by a second volley. Soon, the woods rang with the shots of a full-blown skirmish.

"Sounds like Captain Jewett's got Johnny Reb by the tail," said Irvin. "Forward, men. We must find the Illinois cavalry and get back before we're cut off."

Company K hadn't gone much farther when a second outburst of hot firing reverberated from another location at their rear. "What in tarnation's goin' on back there?" grumbled Keener. "The Gray Fox must be throwin' our boys a surprise party."

Before anyone could reply, Joe saw the Bucktail quar-termaster, Lieutenant Patton, streaking down the lane behind them. Rushing up to Captain Irvin, Patton panted, "Our troops guarding Meadow Bridge. . . were withdrawn by the brass. . . to Beaver Dam Creek. The Rebs crossed the river. . . unopposed. You'd better. . . retreat."

"Are those official orders, Lieutenant?" asked Irvin.

"No, sir. Just my recommendation."

"I'd better maintain my position until official orders arrive," insisted the Captain.

"But you'll be. . . surrounded," sputtered Patton.

"I'll send two of my men back with you to get those orders then. Keener. Jack. Go with the lieutenant. Now!"

"Do I gotta go?" groaned Swift, casting a painful look at Jude and Zack. "Can't I stay here with my brothers?"

"I need two men in case one gets wounded. Get go-ing!"

Lieutenant Patton hustled back down the lane with Joe and Jack close at his heels. The most distant skirmish now seemed to grow fainter and fainter. As the men scrambled along, the firing continued northward until ceasing altogether.

"Sounds like one o' our companies done escaped," puffed Joe.

"Let's hope all of us do," grunted Patton.

"Amen to that," seconded Jack.

The Lieutenant and his couriers sprinted until their lungs wheezed like split bellows. Finally, just ahead, they spotted Company D fighting for their lives against a superior force of Reb infantry. Major Stone personally was directing their retreat through the woods. Patton, Keener, and Swift rushed up to the major to tell him of Company K's plight.

"Too late to help Captain Irvin," said Stone, observing more Rebs spilling up the Meadow Bridge Road. "The only courier that'd reach Irvin now would need a pigeon's wings."

"But what'll happen to Zack and Jude?" screeched Jack, his eyes welling with sudden tears.

"Sorry, son," replied the major, patting the lad on the shoulder. "Fall in and give us a hand getting these other fellows to safety."

"Come on, Jack," said Keener softly, leading the boy to a nearby position in the skirmish line. "Time ta think o' yer own skin."

At Stone's command the Bucktails unleashed a volley that literally blew the Rebs backward. Once Jack sighted down the barrel of his musket, a steely look replaced the tears in his eyes. The shot he fired went straight through the chest of a lean, charging Rebel in a torn butternut jacket.

"Nice shootin'!" crowed Joe. "That'll teach 'im ta tangle with a wildcat pup."

Before the Rebs could regroup, Company D ran fifty yards to a distant patch of woods to reload their weapons. When the Rebs resumed their attack, the Bucktails blasted them with another barrage and again took to their heels.

"Come on!" thundered Joe, yanking Jack to his feet. "Let's git! By the sun, I'd say we's headin' northeast."

"Why, we's goin' back ta Beaver Dam Creek," cried Swift with a relieved grin.

"Ex-actly. Let's fly!"

Keener and Jack tore through the trees until they heard Major Stone blare, "Turn and fight, Bucktails. Give 'em hell!"

When Joe flopped on his belly to face the enemy, he was surprised to find two full regiments of Reb troops swelling from the woods behind him. Their banners flapped menacingly in the breeze as they streamed forward in an unstoppable gray wave.

"Where did all them boys come from?" gasped Jack, peeping over a stump.

"They's reinforcements from that unguarded bridge, laddie. Peddle lead!"

Although Keener and his mates fired and reloaded until their glistening faces blackened with powder smoke, the howling Rebs closed within fifty yards of the Bucktail skirmish line and threatened to overwhelm it. Just then, Keener heard the bright notes of a bugle spill from the woods to his right. In the next instant, a contingent of blue cavalry blasted from concealment and charged on lathered mounts into the teeth of the enemy. The fury of their attack so unnerved the Rebels, that the Bucktails were again able to slip out of the noose.

"Looks like them lost Illinois Cavalry found _us_!" cheered Keener.

"An' jess in time, too!" shouted Swift, waving his cap jubilantly.

Company D sprinted to the top of a small rise, dove to the ground, and fired one lethal volley after another, allowing the cavalry to wheel and escape after them. Jack had now become one with his Springfield. Each time he squeezed the trigger, another Reb threw up his hands and crashed lifelessly to the forest floor. One soldier he shot square in the face. Another he hit through the throat. A third made the mistake of peeking around an oak. Jack took his eye out with a snap shot that made Keener croak, "Laddie, some of the boys call bullets 'swifts.' They musta watched yer shootin' when they come up with that name. How did you jess hit that Reb?"

"Pretended he was my pap."

"Oh!"

With the Confederates milling about in confusion, Stone again ordered Company D to retreat. The riflemen crashed headlong through a heavy thicket that tore at their jackets and left bloody scratches on their hands and faces. Finally, they burst into the margins of a shallow swamp. Beyond the swamp the Union entrenchments, carved into the hillside on the east bank of Beaver Dam Creek, were just visible.

With a weary cheer, the Bucktails splashed through the marsh, clambered down the steep bank of the creek, and waded through chest-deep water to the other even steeper bank. Climbing for all they were worth, they finally reached the Union lines where they scrambled into rifle pits they had dug the day before on the extreme right flank.

Safe at last, Jack collapsed. Lying in the cold loam, his scrawny frame was racked with sobs. His oval face twisted in sorrow. Tears made little rivers through the black powder smoke coating his cheeks.

"Take it easy, laddie," whispered Keener from the next rifle pit. "Weren't no way we coulda helped our company. You saw how many Rebs there was in the woods 'tween them an' us. Be thankful we got away with our hides in one piece."

"But why didn't dang Irvin order a retreat while all the boys still had a chance?"

"He was jess followin' orders, Jack. If he pulled out be-fore he was supposed ta, he coulda got hisself court-martialed. Ed's a brave fella, he is. Ain't gonna back down from no fight."

"W-W-What'll happen ta Zack 'n' Jude if they's cap-tured?"

"End up in a Richmond prison is what. 'Til they's ex-changed."

"Oh, poor Jude! He's already soured by things that done happened ta him. I reckon prison's gonna really bring 'im low."

"It's good o' ya ta worry, Jack. You're mighty close ta them brothers o' yers, ain't ya?"

"Yeah, we was forced ta be close."

"What do ya mean?"

"Our pap's unforgivin' ways made us such. It was us ag'in him from the time we was old e-nough ta do chores 'round the blacksmith shop. We was always black an' blue from his 'correctin'. Jude got the worst o' it, though. He weren't a fast learner like me an' Zack an' got whooped every time Pap had ta ex-plain things more 'n' once ta 'im. That were at least nine er ten times a day."

"No one has it easy, Jack. Jess look at how much trouble I's been in since ya knowed me. The brass figgered Daniel Blett would be a good in-fluence bein' he was the company drillmaster, an' all. That's why I got put in with you boys at Falmouth."

"As big as you is, ya ain't really growed up much, has ya, Joe?" sniffed Jack with a sad smile.

"I ain't much fer responsibilty," replied Keener, flushing as he crawled to the edge of Swift's trench. "Better git some rest now, laddie. Them Rebs was right on our tails when we skedaddled. I'm sure they won't waste no time followin' us here. If ya need ta talk er anything, I'll be listenin'. I reckon you'll have ta settle fer havin' me as a brother. . . 'til Zack an' Jude come back."

"Thanks," said Jack, slapping playfully at the mop of unruly, red hair sticking out from beneath Keener's kepi cap. "Ya might look a lot like a big, old sheep dog, but I reckon you'll have ta do, Joe."

Rebels advance through the woods to cut off the retreat of their Union counterparts during a battle reenactment held at Gargoyle Park in Olean, NY, in September, 2004.

CHAPTER SEVEN:
ATTACK ON BEAVER DAM CREEK

After Joe Keener had calmed down his young friend, Jack, he pulled out his pocket watch and saw that it was two-thirty. He was already exhausted from his escape from the Rebs, and now the heat of the afternoon had become oppressive. The sun baked him. Sweat stung his eyes. His wool uniform itched him in twenty places at once.

Keener wanted to lie down and sleep in the worst way. Instead, he surveyed the Union defenses at Beaver Dam Creek to steel himself for the coming battle. The Federal lines had been reinforced since morning and now included a row of field cannons strung out behind the rifle pits. Back of the Bucktail position, Joe saw the flag of Cooper's Battery fluttering in the midst of four twelve-pounders. Equally reassuring was the presence of two full companies of Berdan's Sharpshooters called up to bolster the First Rifles' ranks. "Played any baseball lately?" chortled Joe when he saw a lanky, green-coated sergeant glaring at him from a nearby trench.

Next, Keener studied the ground the Rebs would have to cross. He knew it well, having marched it twice that day. It was a mixture of woods and swamps with a stream flanked by steep banks. Finally, his eyes stopped on the Cold Harbor Road immediately to his left. The road led to a shallow ford through Beaver Dam Creek. That's where he guessed the Confederates would mass their attack.

Joe continued to gaze off into the distance until he heard footsteps behind him. He turned to see Major Roy Stone striding confidently in his direction. "Bully job today, Private," said Stone. "You and Swift displayed real courage.

I know you'll make fine additions to Company D."

"But what about the boys in Company K?" asked Jack. "Any word, sir?"

"They're still missing is all I know. Take heart, laddie. There haven't been any shots from their last known position. That's a good sign that no harm's come to them."

"Yes, sir."

Suddenly, the major stiffened. Following Stone's eyes, Joe saw a battery of Confederate artillery appear on the high ground beyond the creek and unlimber their cannons. The major scrambled for cover just as another hidden battery farther upstream sent a barrage of shells shrieking over the Bucktail position. There were five separate explosions on the slope between the rifle pits and the Union artillery, followed by the whizzing of shrapnel and a cloud of acrid dust. Two closer barrages came moments later, producing an even heavier shower of blasted dirt.

Keener and Swift flopped face-down and covered their heads with trembling arms until the terrible debris fell short of them and the cannon fire faded away. They had just gotten used to the renewed silence when up the hill behind them Cooper's crew flew into action to answer the Rebs.

Joe watched fascinated as flames spewed from the maws of the twelve-pounders. He flinched at the deafening roar that echoed horribly and watched the field pieces roll back with the concussion. Immediately, the gun crews sprang to push the pieces forward and swab, reload, and fire them. After the thunderous boom of the second bombardment faded away, Keener heard a great cheer rise from the artillery.

"Why's they makin' all that r-r-racket?" stuttered Jack, quivering in the bottom of his trench.

"'Cause there ain't no more Reb shells rainin' on us. Our boys musta made a di-rect hit on their big guns."

Keener again peered out of his rifle pit to find the Rebs swarming onto the Cold Harbor Road. As the Reb attack surged toward them, a battery of Confederate smoothbore cannons opened fire from an opposite patch of woods. The approaching shells shrieked like men rent asunder. Luckily, their low trajectory caused them to thud into the hillside below the Union trenches. Although the barrage missed its mark, Joe could tell by the white faces around him that the shelling was starting to unnerve his comrades.

The Rebels now broke into a run as they advanced like a gray flood toward the ford. They had covered half the distance to Beaver Dam Creek when Cooper's Battery rained shot and shell into their midst. Suddenly, huge gaps appeared in the Confederate ranks. Some men were blown skyward. Others were mowed down like blighted wheat. Yet onward the waving flags advanced, with reserve soldiers pressing forward to fill in the holes in the lines. When the Rebs had closed within a hundred yards, Keener heard Major Stone bellow, "Commence fire!"

The Bucktails and Berdan's sharpshooters unleased a deadly volley that wiped out the entire front line of Confederates. The remaining ranks, stunned by the accuracy of the riflemen's shooting, stumbled to a halt to be raked by a second fusillade of fire. Several Rebs snatched up fallen regimental flags only to be blasted themselves. Finally, the storm of lead became too great. The gray masses reeled and then bolted into the cover of the swampy woodland behind them.

Watching the Berdan men get off three shots to his one with their Sharps breechloaders caused Keener to cuss in frustration. Ramming a Minie ball down the barrel of his Springfield, he snarled, "How does the brass ex-pect us boys ta do our jobs proper when they gives us outdated muskets? It ain't fair that we gotta ex-pose our be-hinds ta the dang Rebs while reloadin' when them snobby U.S. Sharpshooters kin jess lay there an' feed catridge after catridge inta their rifles."

"You're right," said Jack, trembling as he knelt to ram home another round.

"We gotta git us some Sharps o' our own. By hook er by crook."

"Amen ta that."

"What's wrong, laddie? You're shakin' like a dog crappin' peach stones."

"Are you sayin' I'm scared?" snapped Jack, before blowing a retreating Reb off his feet. "I might shoot slower than them Berdan fellas, but I's jess as accurate."

"Nice shooting! By all you men!" whistled Major Stone, coming forward to check on Bucktail casualties. "Those Rebs just melted away!"

After the major returned to his own rifle pit, the Confederates rallied and pushed forward again. This time their assault was more frenzied. Joe could see the determined looks on their powder-blackened faces as they pressed to the very bank of Beaver Dam Creek. A seemingly endless horde charged ahead, trampling underfoot the corpses of their fallen comrades. From the creek to the tree line beyond was a solid roiling mass of gray and butternut bent on destruction. Puffs of smoke rose from individual muskets, and the sun glinted off brandished swords and bayonets.

Joe took a deep breath and then fired his Springfield into the oncoming flood of troops. Glancing to his right, he saw Jack sprawled unmoving in his rifle pit.

"Are ya hit, laddie?" cried Keener. "Laddie?"

"N-o-o... I's jess... ex-hausted."

"Then give me yer catridges, Jack. Now!"

With his ears reddening, Swift crawled to his knees and again reloaded his musket. Soon, he was firing mechanically, oblivious to the Minie balls flying like bees around him.

Joe smiled grimly and blasted a Reb captain directing his company into the breast deep water of Beaver Dam Creek. Incensed, his men waded across the stream and clambered onto the bank directly in front of the Bucktail position. Snarling like rabid curs, they loped up the slope with their Georgia and Louisiana banners flapping defiantly in the breeze. On they rushed, shooting as they came, until Adjutant Hartshorne rallied a contingent of First Rifles and Second Pennsylvania Reserves.

"Fix bayonets!" thundered Hartshorne, drawing his

sword from its scabbard. "Charge!"

While reloading his musket, Keener watched the adjutant's men smash into the Confederate ranks and drive them backward. The fighting was now hand-to-hand and as vicious as any bar brawl Joe had ever been a part of. Bayonets, bowie knives, swords, and fists were wielded with equal fury until the Rebs grudgingly retreated into the now bloody water of Beaver Dam Creek.

The Reserves had just begun dragging their wounded uphill to the shelter of the Union trenches when a scraggly Reb private leveled his musket and sent a ball hurtling toward Ross Hartshorne's skull. There was a spray of gore followed by a surprised cry. As the adjutant slumped wounded to the ground, Jack Swift blew the smirking Reb off his feet with a well-placed shot through the heart. A great hurrah shook the Bucktail lines, and Joe grinned widely at his young brother-in-arms.

Despite mounting casualties, the Confederates continued their desperate assault. The Bucktails fired their muskets until the barrels grew hot and became fouled with black powder. To clear his own weapon, Joe poured water from his canteen down the barrel and swabbed it with a clean cloth hooked to the end of his ramrod. "How many stinkin' Rebs is out there, anyhow?" Keener grumbled. "I swear I seen the battle flags o' three different divisions."

"Dang!" gasped Swift.

"Dang is right! That means we's fightin' two-thirds o' Bobbie Lee's army all by ourselves!"

The Rebs still fired madly into the Bucktail position as the sun dropped below the horizon. Bullets whined harmlessly around the defenders, who mercilessly slaughtered the enemy advancing across open ground. Round after round found its mark until the final Confederate attack sputtered and then collapsed altogether. As the Rebels limped wearily back into the swamp, Joe croaked to Jack, "Looks like it's finally over, laddie. It's a good thing, too, er I'da been chuckin' rocks at 'em pretty soon."

"I'm down ta three catridges myself," sighed Swift.

55

"But listen over yonder. Ain't that more shootin' off ta the left?"

"Yeah, there must be an attack off down the line. I reckon they won't find no weak spot there, neither."

"It's almost dark, anyhow, Joe. It's all gotta end soon with a victory fer us."

"We mighta won the day," muttered Keener, "but I reckon old Bobbie Lee will send his army 'round our right flank be-fore all's said an' done. Then, it'll be our turn ta do the retreatin'."

"I sure hope Adjutant Hartshorne's all right," mumbled Jack. "He sure done a brave thing chargin' them Rebs like that."

"Don't worry 'bout 'im," replied Keener with a quick grin. "Ya don't git ta be a Bucktail officer unless ya got a mighty thick noggin."

"Like Colonel Kane, ya mean?"

"Yeah, who else woulda led a winnin' charge after gettin' blasted in the face. At Dranesville, Kane was a testament ta Bucktail courage jess like the adjutant was here taday."

The strategic placement of an army's artillery batteries, and the accuracy of their fire, often determined the outcome of a Civil War battle. Above, reenactors demonstrate the work done by typical Union cannon crews.

CHAPTER EIGHT:
ANOTHER CLOSE CALL

With the Fourteenth New York called up for picket duty that night, the Bucktails caught some fitful rest in their rifle pits above Beaver Dam Creek. Keener always slept with one eye open, and several times he was disturbed by Jack Swift wrestling with nightmare demons. Finally, Joe hissed, "Wake up, laddie! Wake up be-fore some Reb sniper finds yer position an' sends ya a bumblebee."

"S-S-Sorry," whispered Jack. "I'm always mighty restless when I'm tuckered out. My brothers used ta smack me with straw pillows when I dreamed too much. I reckon yesterday was the hardest day o' my en-tire life."

"Mine, too," Joe said, "an' our fat's still pretty near the fire."

At daybreak, after sorely needed ammunition was issued, word passed down the line that a general retreat had been ordered. First, Joe heard Meade's brigade steal over the rise with a faint clatter of canteens and tin cups. Next, Seymour's boys filed off into the dim light, walking as quietly as their heavy brogans would allow them. Before the Bucktails could join General Reynolds' brigade in their retreat, Major Stone received orders to hold the line until the rest of the army had escaped.

"Why does us boys always git stuck with the dirty work?" grumbled Joe when he heard the news.

"Because we're the best at it," whispered the major testily. "Now, spread out to make the Rebs think all these trenches are occupied."

The Bucktails fanned out to the left and right, and once in position, received orders to open fire on the Rebs. During the night the Confederate artillery had been moved into grapeshot range and commenced a hot reply that sent clusters of small iron balls ripping through the Union defenses. That kept the Bucktails' heads down while the Rebs moved a large contingent of infantry up the Cold Harbor Road. Even worse, the grape made it impossible for the gunners in Cooper's Battery to stand as they attempted to load their field pieces.

Keener watched the Union artillery struggle to answer the Reb big guns. Finally, he bellowed to Jack, "When word comes ta skedaddle, you best do it unless ya wants ta be joinin' yer brothers in Richmond."

"We ain't surrounded yet, Joe," replied Swift, shooting into a clump of gray coats charging toward the ford below. "We jess gotta keep firin'!"

"Yeah, but we'll be flanked soon if Johnny Reb makes it across the creek."

Major Stone must have come to the same conclusion, for soon after he sent Captain Holland and his Company A riflemen scurrying to take up a position directly in front of the shallow crossing place. They immediately poured a volley into a regiment of Rebs splashing through the creek. Bullets tore into the lead soldiers, blowing them backward. As their corpses floated off downstream, the other Rebels found shelter in the trees lining the far bank.

The Bucktails somehow managed to hold the Reb advance in check until a hazy, red sun rose steadily above the horizon. When his cartridge box was nearly empty, Keener saw a courier rush up to Major Stone with new orders. Checking his pocket watch, Joe found it was now six a.m.

"Okay, men," barked Stone. "It's time to retreat."

"Must be the rest o' our boys got clean away," whooped Joe. "Let's fly!"

In order to escape the battlefield, the Bucktails had to cross a half-mile of artillery ravaged hillside in full range of the Reb big guns. At first, Keener and Jack picked their way along by dodging from shell hole to shell hole as cannons banged away on the opposite side of the creek. With the passing of each artillery storm, up they jumped until another barrage sent them diving on their bellies.

"Might as well try hittin' a r-r-runnin' rabbit as Jack Swift," chattered the lad nervously after a particularly close call.

"Er a bull with wings in my case," added Keener. "Come on. Git goin'."

Jack and Joe leaped to their feet and sprinted even faster than before. Several times fountains of earth rained down debris near the racing soldiers. More often, the rough ground sent them sprawling on their faces, raising painful bruises on their legs and knees. The morning had become frightfully muggy, too, and by the time they reached safety, they dropped exhausted in a growing circle of panting Bucktails.

When Major Stone finally crossed the dangerous ground, he said, "We've still got one more thing to do to slow up the Rebs. Captain Wister, I want you to take Company B to the Mill Hospital and destroy the bridge there."

"Where's that, sir?" asked the captain, his sharp eyes blazing.

"It's only a few hundred yards downstream on the Ellerson's Mill Road. You can't miss it. Good luck, Langhorne. I know you'll do whatever's necessary."

"Thank you, sir!"

After Langhorne Wister's men had filed off through the trees, Keener heard gunfire echo from Beaver Dam Creek behind them. Painfully crawling to his feet, he stared down the hill until spotting a small group of Bucktails hotly engaging an entire Reb division.

"Who's that?" asked Joe. "They sure got a gator by the tail."

"That's Captain Niles," replied Major Stone. "He was supposed to have retreated with the rest of us. I hope his orders reached him. Look, he's leading his company into that swamp. He'll keep the Rebs playing hide-and-seek a long time there."

"But isn't that the Bucktail banner he's got with him?" gasped Jack.

"Let's hope he hides it good if he's captured," said Keener. "I reckon them Rebs would sell their own mamas inta slavery ta git a hold o' that flag!"

"Okay, let's move out!" barked Stone. "We must reach Gaines' Mill before the Rebs do!"

With a low groan, the Bucktails struggled into formation and marched east toward a highland just visible on the north bank of the Chickahominy River. The pace quickened when a shadowy group of Reb skirmishers appeared suddenly on their flank and began dogging the Bucktails' retreat. Soon, puffs of musket smoke rose from the trees on both sides of the First Pennsylvania Rifles, sending them sprinting toward the distant Federal lines.

The blazing sun became so intense that many men couldn't keep pace. When they fell behind, squads of Rebels swooped from the brush to capture them. Others fell victim to heat exhaustion and fainted from the ranks. Jack Swift was one of them. When his legs melted from beneath him, Joe gathered the lad into his massive arms and slung him over his shoulder like a sack of potatoes. The other sick men lay where they fell, also to be taken into custody by the gray vultures hovering in the brush.

Burdened by the extra weight of his young friend, Keener soon struggled to keep up with the column. Finally, a lanky cold-eyed Berdan sergeant grunted, "Leave that whelp lay, Private. No use losing a brawler like you to save his worthless hide."

"Who you callin' 'worthless'?" snarled Joe. "Jack's fought jess as hard as any man de-spite losin' his two brothers. I ain't leavin' him be-hind no matter what ya say!"

"Yeah, you're doin' the right thing," affirmed a nearby Bucktail sergeant. "Carry on!"

Keener judged that the Bucktails covered a good five miles before sighting the Union entrenchments built in a semi-circle around a tall farmhouse just visible through the trees. After wiping the sweat from his eyes with a big paw, Joe saw that the Union left occupied some high ground near the Chickahominy River. The rest of the line followed a sickle-shaped stream cutting through a wooded bog back to the river on the right. Several bridges connected the army with the southern bank behind the dug-in troops. No breastworks had been thrown up, and Joe figured that axes must not have been available to further fortify the otherwise strong position.

The Bucktails tramped wearily through a regiment of General Morrell's division posted on the left flank. Joe could see General McCall's men, held in reserve, were spread out about six hundred yards beyond the front line. The scorching sun had reached its zenith, and Keener thankfully collapsed in the shade of the woods occupied by the other Pennsylvania Volunteer Regiments. He lay Jack at the base of a large oak and unbuttoned the boy's jacket. He wet his handkerchief with water from his canteen. Afterward, Keener mopped the soggy cloth across Jack's burning forehead until the lad's eyes fluttered open.

"W-W-Where am I?" croaked Jack, struggling to sit up.

"Set still, laddie. We's made it ta Gaines' Mill."

"You mean we ain't captured?"

"No, son, we's safe. . . fer now."

Joe offered Jack a swig from his canteen, and soon the boy was dozing peacefully in the shade. Keener sat with his back against the tree next to his friend. He immediately fell into an exhausted sleep and knew nothing until the steady pop of small arms fire crept into his consciousness two hours later.

Joe woke with a start to find the Rebs smashing into the Union left flank. The assault was so ferocious that gray coated squads could be seen pouring through holes blown in the blue ranks. Each time the Confederates breached the line, Reserve Corps soldiers sprang forward to plug the gaps. Muskets were shot at point-blank range with telling effect, and piles of dead soon littered the blood-soaked ground.

Keener had little time to witness this carnage when

Major Stone shouted for the Bucktails and Berdan Sharpshooters to fall into line. The burly private shook Jack awake and helped him wobble to his feet. The lad took another swig of water from his own canteen before planting a brave smile on his face. "Let's git at it!" cried Swift. "There's work ta be done!"

Major Stone rallied his depleted regiment of 150 survivors. Yanking his revolver from its shiny leather holster, he charged forward to the center of the Union line. The Rebs now began a full-scale attack along the entire Yankee front, and the thunder of muskets and artillery became deafening. The Bucktails flopped into shallow rifle pits and banged away at an infantry regiment hidden in some woods that Keener judged to be 500 yards distant. A Rebel battery sat out in the open there, and Jack began picking off a cannon crew one-by-one until the artillerymen scrambled to roll their field guns out of range. The newly placed cannons bellowed only a couple more times before the gunners learned the hard way that they hadn't moved far enough to escape Swift's lethal aim. They were forced twice more to relocate, chased by the lad's deadly fire.

"That's showin' 'im, Jackie boy!" yelled Keener. "It's a good thing ya ain't fully rested, er there wouldn't be one o' them cannoneers left standin'! Are ya holdin' up okay?"

"You bet, Joe. If my eyes don't glaze over, I'll be jess dandy."

The Bucktails kept at their deadly work until almost out of ammunition. When their shooting slowed, the Rebs poured out of the woods and rushed into rank to sweep the First Rifles from the field. Propelled forward by the rebel yell, they formed a seemingly endless wave of gray destruction.

"Okay, steady, men," ordered Major Stone. "Load. Fire!"

The Bucktail rifles cracked in unison, and smoke and flames belched from their barrels. When the smoke had cleared, a great carnage had chewed up the Reb ranks. Dead lay sprawled on their faces up and down the line. The cries of the wounded replaced defiant howls. Before the enemy could recover, the Fifth Pennsylvania Reserves leaped from their entrenchments and sprinted to within 150 yards of the reeling gray ranks to rake them with another potent volley.

Jack's shrill cheer accompanied the Rebels when they broke and ran back into the wooded swamp. He and Joe exchanged handshakes and then waved their hats jubilantly in the air. They continued to celebrate until a fresh mass of Confederates was seen pressing forward all along the front.

"Ain't there no end ta these Rebs?" cried Swift.

"Not with Stonewall Jackson joinin' the party," groaned Keener. "Ain't that him jess over yonder bringin' up more troops?"

Joe and Jack crawled back into their rifle pits to watch the Union lines collapse around them. Bravely, the Bucktails continued to blast away at the advancing Rebs until a nasty barrage ripped up their right flank. Keener turned to find a hostile force in ragged butternut streaming to engulf them through a hole in the overrun Yankee position there.

To prevent another round of enfilading fire, Major Stone barked, "Wheel, men, wheel! Load! Commence!"

The Bucktail volley was delivered into the very face of the enemy, temporarily stemming the butternut tide. Before the Bucktails could reload, shells from their own artillery began raining around them sending up plumes of shattered earth.

"Fall back!" commanded Stone. "Retreat!"

The Bucktails threaded their way through a blue throng pushing toward the rear. They soon came to a shortened Union line held by Meagher's and French's brigades. Without panic, they passed through these defenses and reformed behind a makeshift hospital.

The First Rifles, receiving permission to fall out of rank, slumped spent to the ground. With a low whistle, Keener pointed to a road leading from downriver to the bridges directly behind them. The road was completely jammed with a long line of supply wagons from White House Landing. The vehicles groaned beneath the weight of food, ammunition, and baggage. The mule drivers, frustrated by the bogged down traffic, filled the air with vile curses that made Jack cringe. Adding to the confusion on the road were stalled caissons, moan-filled ambulances, walking wounded, and stragglers from untold broken regiments.

Finally, Joe saw W. H. D. Hatton, the Bucktail chaplain, stride onto the road to direct traffic. With firm patience, he ordered the companies of lost, milling men to stand aside. Then, he discovered an overloaded wagon with a broken axle that he ordered some stragglers to unload and drag into a field. This opened a lane for the stalled ambulances to squeeze through. Once the ambulances no longer blocked the way, the wagons proceeded in an orderly fashion over the opened bridges.

"If Hatton kin git a man inta heaven as easy as he done untangled that traffic," chortled Joe, "then I want that fella near me when I catch a dang Reb bullet."

"That's nothin' ta joke about," warned Jack, "especially fer a whiskey swillin' fella like you. I don't take much stock in all that fancy preachin' stuff myself. I know God'll take care o' me as long as I lives like He wants me ta. I jess wish you'd give up some o' them bad ways o' yers, Joe, 'cause there ain't a fella I'd rather enter them Pearly Gates with than you."

"Thanks, laddie, but I reckon a spotted dog will carry them spots ta the grave no matter how often his master washes 'em."

"Enough of that kind of talk," growled Major Stone, overhearing the soldiers' morbid conversation. "Okay, Bucktails, time to move out."

The major marched the regiment to a meadow near one of the bridges and then left with Captain Wister in tow. As Stone strode purposefully away, Joe heard him mutter, "Rumor has it that General Reynolds got captured. We'd better corral as many of the Pennsylvania Reserves as we can, Captain, to protect the wagons until they've crossed the river."

"Yes, sir!"

In the fading light, clumps of soldiers began filing to the meadow to join the Bucktails. Many were hatless. Others carried no rifles. Most wore a defeated or confused look as they stumbled in to join up with the other Pennsylvania Reserves. Their ranks continued to swell until Keener judged that over 2,000 worn-out soldiers had assembled around him. At two in the morning, Major Stone ordered them into marching formation, and they tramped over the swaying bridge to the southern bank of the Chickahominy River.

"Do I look as bad as the rest o' these here fellas?" yawned Keener as they began their retreat.

"Worse," grinned Jack. "But bein' you're so big an' ugly, I won't have ta worry 'bout losin' ya in the dark."

CHAPTER NINE:
SAVAGE STATION

The Bucktails marched south all night behind a huge bellowing herd of army beef cattle driven along the road ahead by cussing cavalry. The muddy byway was made slicker by cattle dung and the impact of thousands of hooves. The First Rifles were completely covered with muck by the time they arrived the following morning at the artillery park commanded by General H. J. Hunt.

"Why, all I kin see is yer eyes," chortled Keener when he caught his first glimpse of Jack at daylight.

Instead of replying, Swift burst into tears. He sobbed uncontrollably until the Bucktails were dismissed from rank and Joe said, "Come on, laddie, set down by this row o' cannon. I reckon we'll be here fer a while 'til the brass figgers where ta send us next. I hope it's straight ta the James River so we kin wash our dang uniforms. We got so much mud caked on us, we look 'xactly like the dirty Rebs."

Keener collapsed next to a twelve-pound field gun and pulled some paper and a pen from his knapsack. After glancing around to study the thirteen batteries of cannons parked around him, Joe began scribbling like crazy. Jack, who had been busy washing his face with water from his canteen, finally asked, "What's ya doin? Drawin' pitchers?"

"Nah! I figgered I best write Hosea Curtis an' let 'im know how we's doin'. We's been so busy fightin' an' retreatin' that I plumb fergot ta answer his last letter."

"Fightin' an' retreatin' is right!" cried Swift, again breaking down. "I'm too tuckered out ta go another step."

"Now. Now. It ain't so bad com-pared ta what Hosea's squad jess done. Don't ya remember how they drove the Rebs the en-tire length o' the Shenandoah Valley? What we been through's a walk down the main street o' Curwensville com-pared ta that. Want ta hear what I wrote 'bout our battles?"

"I g-g-guess so. . . "

"Okay. You listen real close, an' let me know if I left anything out:

Howdy Hosea,

I heared Old Jack took you fellas ta the woodshed and whipped yer behinds good fer ya out there in the Shenandoah. Well, there's more than a few sore rears here in the Peninsula, too. Only us boys got whopped by that old schoolmaster, Robert E. Lee.

Down here we got ourselves in one terrible tussle after another. At Beaver Dam Creek we damn near got captured, and at Gaines' Mill a whole division of Rebs was looking ta grind us inta meal. Let me tell ya, we paid them back in their own coin. I fired until my gun got so hot, I scalded two charging Rebs ta death with it. When I run outta bullets, the air got so thick with my cussing, the Confederate attack couldn't break through. We got clean away while they waited fer the wind ta thin out the air some.

Well, Hosea, I'll let ya git back ta licking yer wounds. I hear a plan's in the works ta reunite us Bucktails. Them generals better hurry, er all they'll be getting from our regiment will be one good company. We gotta learn not ta fight so hard, er we'll become scarcer than hair on General Burnside's noggin.

Joe Keener

P.S. Tell that Boone fella ta hand in his jester's cap because he's met his match."

The tears dried on Jack's face as he listened to Keener's epistle. Soon, his wide mouth stretched into a rubbery smile. By the time Joe had finished reading, the lad shook with uncontrollable laughter.

"Well?" said Joe coyly. "Did I leave anything out?"

"Only the part 'bout you bein' the biggest liar in Mr. Lincoln's en-tire army. If you wrote the company reports insteada Major Stone, every one o' us would git the Metal o' Honor them Congressmen's close ta passin' fer us army boys."

"Thank you. Thank you."

"Who's that Boone fella, anyhow?"

"Oh, Boone Crossmire's in Company I. He fancies hisself the regimental joker. I can't wait ta trade yarns with that boy. After I give 'im a few volleys, he'll be wavin' the white flag."

"That I'd like ta see."

Joe and Jack exchanged grins and then Keener asked, "How come a bright lad like you can't do no readin' o' yer own?"

"Pap kept us boys too busy firin' up his forge, workin' his bellows, luggin' iron, an' such. He took no stock in book learnin'. He said that was fer sissies."

"Well, I ain't no sissy. Would ya like me ta learn ya ta write yer name?"

"Sure!"

"Okay, ya gotta start with the letter J that's formed like so. Now, you try it."

Swift took the pen from Joe and wrote a perfect letter on his first attempt. "That J kinda looks like a fish hook, don't it?" he said. "That'll make it easy ta remember. Is that the same letter starts yer name?"

"You bet! What a fast learner you is!"

"What's the second letter o' my name?"

"It's an A, an' it's writ like so."

Again Jack perfectly copied the letter written by Keener and then asked him to spell out his full name. He also got this on the first try. Afterward, he filled up a whole sheet of paper with the word "Jack."

"How 'bout my last name?" jabbered Swift. "Kin ya teach me that? Huh? Huh?"

"When we git ta our new base, I'll give ya all the lessons ya want," grinned Joe. "I think it best now that we git some rest while we kin."

"I guess you're right," sighed Jack. "Maybe when we git where we're goin', my brothers won't be lost no more, an' you kin learn them, too."

"I sure will. Now, lay down, laddie, an' catch yerself a few winks."

Keener and Swift lay in the shade of the big cannon and fell instantly asleep. They snored peacefully until just before dark. They awoke to the sound of Major Stone's shouting and the crack of distant thunder. With a groan, they struggled to their feet and shuffled sleepily into marching formation. A few drops of rain began falling from the threatening skies to further dampen their spirits.

When the regiment was assembled, the major said with evident pride, "Men, the Pennsylvania Reserve Corps has been assigned a very important task by General McClellan himself. Because of our bravery at Beaver Dam Creek, where we gave up not one inch of ground to the Rebs, Little Mac has asked us to escort General Hunt's artillery through White Oak Swamp. It's imperative that the artillery gets through and sets up on high ground to protect the retreat. Are you up to this task, men?"

"Yes, sir," droned the exhausted soldiers.

"Are you sure?"

"Yes, sir!"

"Okay, let's move out!"

The Bucktails joined a long line of groaning battery wagons, ammunition trains, and caissons hauling sleek field guns. The column, which stretched out for seven miles, creaked in motion just after dark as rain poured down in sheets. Travel was slowed by the slick roads and the blackness of the night. The heavy train soon turned the narrow route into a series of treacherous mud holes that frustrated the mules, drivers, and their accompanying guards alike.

"Why in tarnation does the army travel so much at

night?" grumbled Jack while skidding through the mud.

"Ta keep Johnny Reb in the dark," replied Keener. "We don't want old Bobbie Lee knowin' where we're goin', do we?"

"N-o-o. But it sure would help if I could see where I was goin'!"

The three hundred vehicles of General Hunt's reserve artillery continued to crawl south all night. Often, the wagons bogged down in the slop and had to be pushed forward by the cursing Pennsylvania troops. By daylight, the men and mules had about reached the limit of their endurance.

Still the artillery column pushed on until the white buildings surrounding a railroad station gleamed through the trees. Here, the Bucktails were greeted by a ghastly sight. Beyond a sign that named the train stop "Savage Station," lay a multitude of bleeding Union casualties. Everywhere bandaged men lay on stretchers and in ambulances. Others could be seen through the open doorways of barns, feed stores, and even outhouses. To Jack it seemed that their groaning came from everywhere at once.

Before orders to fall out had been given, Swift and many other Pennsylvania Reserves bolted from the ranks and began feverishly searching for their fallen comrades. "Jude!" cried Jack. "Zack! Are you here? Please be here!"

Swift returned to his place in line an hour later with tears streaming down his face. "So yer brothers are still missin'?" asked Joe kindly when the boy came stomping dejectedly back through the mud.

"Yeah. . . an' I looked everywhere. . . "

"That's a lot o' lookin' with over two regiments' worth o' wounded layin' about."

"But, Lord, why couldn't they have been here?"

"Maybe that's a good thing, Jack. If ya didn't find 'em, they most likely still got two good legs. An' how are these boys gonna git moved? We sure can't take 'em, an' no Union train's goin' up this track ag'in any time soon. That means the Reb'll git 'em."

"You're. . . right. I jess miss my brothers so much that any news would be welcome. . . "

"The best news I could git is when ta ex-pect a rations wagon. I ain't swallowed nothin' but my own spit fer two days."

"Yeah, I could even stand some embalmed beef 'bout now."

"How about some fresh dog meat?" growled the same Berdan corporal whose nose Keener had broken in Falmouth.

The U.S. Sharpshooter came trooping from a deserted outbuilding carrying a squirming mongrel by the scruff of the neck. When he rejoined the lanky, cold-eyed sergeant from his outfit, the men held down the yelping hound, while another Berdan soldier drew his bayonet to slit the animal's throat. Before the third Sharpshooter could carry out his mission, the dog planted its teeth in the sergeant's hand. With a cry, he loosened his grip, and the hound squirmed free. The men lunged to catch him, but the dog darted away and scooted to Jack. Jack scooped the scrawny hound into his arms while the Sharpshooters rose cursing from the mud.

"Give us that dog, kid," growled the corporal with the broken nose, "or we'll roast you instead."

"No! You stay away!"

"We found that rascal, and finders is keepers where we come from!" snarled the sergeant.

"Ain't you boys from New York City?" asked Keener, stepping to block the path of the lanky soldier.

"What of it?"

"You city folks might use dogs fer food, but in our neck o' the woods we use 'em ta find what we eats! As such, that hound is a lot more valuable ta the regiment, so back off!"

"Why should I?"

"Because I order it," said Major Stone, who had watched the whole incident. "The last thing we need is more men laying in stretchers with Bobbie Lee's whole army breathing down our necks. Now, get back in line. We're about to move out!"

After the column again set in motion, Joe said with a

smirk, "I reckon when that Shakespeare fella wrote 'bout unleashin' the dogs o' war, he weren't referrin' ta that sorry mongrel. Why, he looks like the cross 'tween a coon an' the hound that chases it."

"Then why did ya save 'im if ya thinks he's so ugly?" asked Jack with a hurt look.

"Now, don't git yer back up. I was only funnin' ya. I reckon yer dog'll make a dandy mascot fer us Bucktails."

"Really?"

"Sure! The 102nd Pennsylvany Regiment's got one, so why shouldn't we? They call their dog 'Jack,' but that name's already taken."

"Then what should we name 'im?"

"He's a scrawny fella. Why don't we call 'im 'Little Mac'?"

"Yeah, but wouldn't General McClellan git sore if we done stole his nickname an' give it ta a dog?"

"Maybe you're right. How 'bout 'Boone' after Hosea's Private Crossmire? I'll bet Crossmire's got a face that makes our little friend look like the blue ribbon winner at the county fair."

"That's a good one," snickered Jack. "Boone it is!"

"Hey, ya best not hold Boone that tight, laddie."

"Why not? Do ya think I'll hurt 'im?"

"No, but I'm afraid you'll give 'im yer fleas!"

Dogs were a common sight around Civil War camps. Once accustomed to the fearful noise of combat, many mascots followed their regiments into battle.

CHAPTER TEN:
STOPPING THE REBS

The Bucktails slogged along guarding the artillery train until it passed through White Oak Swamp. The road here was even more treacherous than the one to Savage Station, and many times Joe Keener was asked to put his broad shoulders against a bogged down battery wagon to work it free. Jack, meanwhile, carried his floppy eared friend and Joe's rifle whenever the big private pushed and grunted.

The column crept along to the calls of alarmed crows and swamp creatures until late afternoon. When the artillery finally gained solid ground, the Bucktails and the other Pennsylvania Reserves were ordered down what Joe overheard Major Stone to say was New Market Road.

"Why'd we leave the cannons?" asked Jack.

"I reckon ta head off the Rebs," replied Joe. "Bobbie Lee's most likely comin' from Richmond ta the west an' would like nothin' better than ta cut the Union wagon train in two. Then he could roll up our en-tire army!"

"We can't let that happen!" cried Swift.

"Dang right!"

Joe and Jack marched with new resolve until they were ordered to fall out just before dark near the intersection of Quaker Road with the main highway. With the location of the enemy unknown, Major Stone ordered pickets to form on the camp's perimeter. "The rest of you boys rest on your rifles," he cautioned, "but don't sleep. Roll up your right sleeves in case of a night fight. That way we'll know friend from foe."

Keener and Swift flopped on their bellies behind a rough barked hickory and peered around opposite sides of the trunk toward the west. Their adopted hound shivered between them as if anticipating disaster. Crickets shrilled in the dark, and frogs croaked from unseen swamps. Several times word passed down the line to stay alert, but the only incursion that threatened the Federal position was made by fireflies that glowed eerily in the dark wood.

When the first signs of dawn streaked the sky, Jack nodded sleepily to Keener and said, "Boy, that sure was a long night. I really had ta fight hard ta stay awake, an' fer what?"

"Ta make ya too tired ta fight taday," groused Joe. "Another great de-cision made by the brass."

At seven a.m. a courier brought orders for Major Stone, and the Bucktails again trod cautiously down the New Market Road with the rest of the Pennsylvania Reserve Division. Keener could see General McCall riding ahead on his dapple-gray mount surveying the distance with a set of field glasses. The morning was perfectly calm and cloudless, and the general's head bobbed excitedly at what he saw. Stretched out directly in front of them, even Keener knew was the perfect place to engage the enemy. A clearing over 1,000 yards long and 800 yards wide provided an unobstructed view for their army to train their guns on. The left flank was protected by thick woods and a small farmhouse. The right flank was formed by the road itself bordered by more timberland. Behind them ran a wooded slope that would be easy to defend if they were pushed back.

Joe grinned widely when orders came for the troops to spread into battle formation. Boone seemed genuinely pleased, too, by the way he pranced and barked as the troops assumed their places in the blue line. In front of the infantry four batteries of cannons were wheeled into position to better rake the flat, open ground before them.

The Bucktails and Berdan Sharpshooters were placed in reserve on the left flank. The morning had become hotter, and sweat poured from the mop of red hair curling out from beneath Keener's cap. He stood numbly waiting for the Rebs, taking frequent pulls on his canteen. He wished Major

Stone weren't so close, so he could drink from the flask he had hidden in his coat pocket. Finally, he mumbled to Jack, "It's hotter 'n' the fire we's gonna pour on them Rebs. How ya holdin' up, laddie?"

"I'm gettin' sleepier an' sleepier," replied Swift, bending to give his hound a pat on the head. "I'm so tired, my face feels kinda prickly. An' my arm's asleep from holdin' my musket fer so long."

"Hang in there, Jack. Look. The Twelfth Pennyslvany's bein' advanced. Should be some action soon."

As Keener watched, six companies of the Twelfth Regiment swarmed past the Union battery ahead and rushed forward to the protection of a log farmhouse and a rail fence near the woods. Once these soldiers were in place, all grew quiet again as the oppressive heat discouraged any unnecessary movement.

When the heat had all but drained the last of Keener's energy, the distant boom of artillery jarred his consciousness. Pulling listlessly at his watch chain, Joe saw that it was a few minutes after two. There wasn't much time to ponder this discovery. The next instant he was diving to escape the whistling of shells, the dull thud of exploded earth, and the shriek of shrapnel.

The second bombardment was even closer, causing Boone to yip, yip, yip and break for the wooded ridge behind them. Jack leaped up to catch him but was immediately yanked from his feet by Keener.

"What'd ya do that fer?" cried Swift, nursing a bruised elbow. "I-I-I was jess gettin' ta like that dog!"

"Do ya wanna git yerself killed? Let 'im go! If I had as much sense as him, I'd run, too!"

The Union field guns sprang into action to answer the Rebs shot for shot until the horrific howl of the rebel yell announced the enemy's presence in the woods near the Twelfth Pennsylvania. Joe saw that the Confederate artillery was pummeling the Twelfth. The Federal batteries, though, were totally ineffective. Their shots fell well wide of the charging gray force pressing forward to annihilate anything in its path.

"Look at them Virginians come!" exclaimed Joe, pointing to the Rebels pouring out of the underbrush.

"They's mighty tough targets dodgin' an' comin' double-quick!" screeched Jack.

"Our cannoneers sure think so. Look at how lousy they're firin' them big guns o' theirs!"

Explosion after explosion rocked the log house and rail barricade until blue bodies littered the yard. The surviving infantry poured three volleys into the charging Virginians, who had grown bolder with the Union artillery's bad shooting. When the Yankee cannon crews then broke and ran, the Rebs howled like blood-crazed wolves and rushed to surround the Twelfth Pennsylvanians.

"Look! Now, our infantry's runnin'!" cried Jack.

"It's either that er git captured," yelped Keener. "Somebody better stop them stinkin' Virginians!"

At that moment General McCall galloped up on his horse and bellowed, "Colonel Simmons, take your Fifth Regiment forward and see if you can plug that breech in our line! And get those craven gunners back to work! Move out!"

Simmons' regiment, snarling with rage, fixed bayonets and charged headlong into the advancing Rebs. They hit them with such force that the gray ranks were stopped cold. The grizzled warrior, Simmons, swung wildly with his sword, hacking down Reb after Reb. He continued to deal death until a point-blank shot to the chest sent him crashing to the ground. With the demise of their leader, Keener heard an angry growl rise from the charging Yanks, and they slashed and smashed with even greater fury until the Reb line buckled and broke. A host of Rebs threw down their weapons and surrendered rather than taste cold steel.

The cheers of the victorious Fifth had barely reached Jack and Joe when a fresh wave of Rebs spilled out of the woods and crashed into the surprised Pennsylvania infantry. The Fifth broke and ran just as the Bucktails were sent forward to help them. The Union artillery ran again, too, and

Major Stone now saw a panicked mob bearing down on his regiment.

"Lay down, Bucktails," commanded Stone. "Now!"

To avoid getting pushed down, the Bucktails fell on their faces. Stone shouted for the fleeing Yankees to stop and fight, but on they stampeded with fear glittering in their eyes. Then Captain Holland leaped up in front of a squad of retreating men and shouted, "Halt! Halt! Rally! Rally!" When his entreaties went unheeded, he attempted to stop another group of cowards. Before he could block their path, a Reb Minie ball slammed into his forehead and sent him tumbling to the ground. Splattered with Holland's blood, the throng of soldiers ran even faster for the safety of the rear.

Once the rabble had retreated over them, the Bucktails sprang up and poured a murderous volley into the oncoming Rebel horde. Although their fire took a deadly toll, the gray ranks kept coming like a howling, angry sea. A storm of shot and shell ripped through the First Rifles, and one-by-one they spun lifeless to the ground. The gray sea poured in from three sides when Major Stone finally shouted, "Fall back, men! Before we're surrounded."

Joe Keener blasted another charging Reb. Afterward, he glanced about to locate his young friend, Jack. The lad's hat was missing, and blood oozed from a jagged hole in the left shoulder of his blue coat. With his eyes glazed with pain and fatigue, Jack toppled backward when he tried to stand.

Joe grasped Swift by the collar and began dragging him backward. As they moved crab-like from the battlefield, two scrawny Rebs thrusting bayonet-pointed muskets rushed to cut them off. The enemy closed to within five yards before Jack, with the last energy he could muster, blasted the lead Rebel off his feet. The other charged snarling only to be smashed in the face by a left hook from Keener's massive fist. The musket clattered to the ground, and the Reb, falling on his own bayonet, wailed a high-pitched death cry.

The Bucktails retreated in good order for another four hundred yards as the Rebs veered off to attack a larger Union contingent. In the rear, Major Stone found bits and pieces of several broken regiments milling around without one officer to lead them. With the battle still raging off to the right, Stone shouted, "Men, we must get into formation and help our beleaguered comrades. Are you with me, men? Are you?"

Stone drew himself up to his full height. Fire shot from his dark eyes. His dark hair and powder-blackened face and uniform made his stern resolve even more imposing. Soon, squad after squad began rallying to his fierce, repeated entreaties.

While the Bucktail major was assembling his new force, Joe dragged Jack into a gully to examine his wound. The boy had fainted from exhaustion, and Keener was not far from it himself. He exhaled a great sigh when he found his friend's shoulder had only been grazed by a Reb ball. Afterward, he collapsed panting to the ground to wash Jack's cut skin with the last of the water from his canteen.

Joe was about to sink into unconsciousness until the rush of flying feet had him furiously reloading his musket. He whipped his gun to his shoulder and steadily squeezed the trigger. The intruder was only a few yards from the lip of the gully and coming fast. Keener aimed through his sights and held his breath in anticipation. His finger tightened on the trigger. Closer. Closer.

At the last instant, Joe released his grip and emitted a relieved chortle. Into the gully exploded Boone, madly wagging his tail. He bounded over to Jack and licked the boy's face until his eyes fluttered open. "Boone," he wheezed. "Is that you? Oh, it's so good ta see ya."

"So you are gonna sur-vive?" chuckled Keener. "You lay still here with your pal. I gotta go back an' help the major."

"Ya mean the battle ain't over? Why, it's almost. . . dark."

"Lay still. Ya hear? I'll be back. I promise."

Joe crawled wearily to his feet and clawed his way to the top of the gully. Afterward, he staggered toward Major Stone's new command. The battle flags of six different regiments fluttered amid the ranks, and the looks on the soldiers' faces mirrored their commander's determination. Keener stumbled into line just as the soldiers began marching back toward the action.

It was only minutes before dark when the reserves arrived at the original battle line. The field was scattered with wrecked cannons and corpses in blue and gray. The Reb fire had stopped completely, and Major Stone wondered aloud, "Where in tarnation did those Rebels go? They couldn't have broken through, or we'd hear shooting from the wagon trains behind us."

"Where did they go?" came a raspy voice behind the major. "That's what I intend to discover!"

Stone turned to see the mounted General McCall trot alone from the dusk. The general's left arm dangled uselessly from a bullet he had taken there. "Coming, Major?" he asked.

"Yes, sir!"

Major Stone leaped on a horse that had been wandering close by and followed McCall west down the New Market Road. They just cantered around a sharp bend and disappeared when Joe Keener heard a renewed burst of musket fire. Joe gazed intently through the growing gloom. One rider, he immediately recognized as the Bucktail commander, came galloping back to growl madly for his men to fan out and prepare to meet the enemy.

"Stand fast," commanded Stone. "I'm off to get us some artillery."

The major had only ridden a short ways when he slumped forward over the horse's neck. His mount slowed to a trot before stopping altogether. Keener and several other Bucktails rushed to pull Stone from the saddle. They found blood gushing from a wound in the major's hand.

"Bandage 'im up!" thundered Keener. "Let's git 'im ta the hospital."

"They captured the general," croaked Stone. "Are they coming? Coming?"

"No, sir," replied Joe. "It's too dark fer them Rebs ta

fight more taday. You re-lax whiles we gets ya ta a doctor."

"Yeah, rest easy," said another Bucktail. "We stopped them Rebs, sure as shootin'. That'll give our wagons another whole night ta git safe ta the James River."

CHAPTER ELEVEN:
SAFE AT LAST

Joe Keener groped through the dark and almost fell into the gully where he had left Jack. Only Boone's warning bark kept him from pitching headlong into the greater darkness below. Carefully, Joe climbed to the bottom with Boone's sudden whimpering to guide him. There he found Jack snoring peacefully with his dog cradled in his arms.

"Good thing ya re-cognized my scent, boy," whispered Keener, patting the regiment's new mascot on the head. "Jack. Jack. Wake up, son."

The boy moaned softly but did not stir until Joe shook him firmly by the shoulder. "Get up!" hissed Keener. "Er you'll be left be-hind with the rest o' the wounded!"

Jack finally mumbled, "H-H-Help me. Will ya? I feel so w-w-weak."

Keener pulled his young friend to his feet and then steadied him as he hobbled to the side of the gully. "If ya stand on my shoulders, laddie," advised Joe, "you'll be able ta reach the top. Go on, now. Ya gotta try."

Keener leaned against the damp earth wall and braced himself. With all the effort he could muster, Jack climbed Joe like a ladder. He rose tottering on Joe's shoulders and then painfully pulled himself out of the gully. His dog scampered after him, sending dirt and rocks down on Keener as he clawed cussing to safety. When Joe finally emerged from the hole, he said, "Why in thunder did ya leave yer gun down there? No way them Rebs is done with us yet."

"Don't worry," panted Jack. "I'll find one. There's plenty o' muskets scattered 'round after taday's battle."

With Keener's help, Swift staggered toward a shadowy

column forming up on the road to their right. Just before they arrived, they stumbled over some corpses, and Jack yelped, "My shins jess barked ag'in a gun stock. Pick that musket up fer me, will ya, Joe? That dead fella has no more use fer it."

Using his new gun for a crutch, Jack hobbled into formation flanked by Keener and Boone. Soon after, the column lurched into motion, and Joe heard the soldier next to him grumble, "This is the third night in a row we ain't gonna git no sleep. No wonder so many o' the boys run taday. We's all too tuckered out ta fight."

"Speak fer yerself," grunted Keener. "A lot o' men we left lyin' back yonder fought ta the death de-spite the little rest they got."

The Bucktails joined a larger group of Pennsylvania Reserves gathered at a crossroads and turned south for an all-night march. Keener stumbled along rotely, concentrating on putting one foot in front of the other. Several times he was conscious of soldiers crashing out of line like felled trees. When the first light of morning illuminated the road around him, he found only sixty Bucktails still present in the ranks.

Now, Jack was really floundering. He couldn't take more than a few weak steps at a time before stopping to rest. Finally, Keener hoisted the lad over his shoulder and trudged purposefully onward. The road led to a distant summit that dominated the landscape. As the Pennsylvania Reserves limped closer, Keener could see this hill was alive with Union activity. Slopes devoid of trees and brush led upward to tier after tier of cannons that stretched all the way to the top. On the summit itself, Joe saw massive siege guns poised to rain destruction on the Rebels.

"Look up yonder, Jack," said Keener with a low whis-tle. "Why, there must be 200 big guns on that hill. An' look at them breastworks and all them divisions o' blue coats swarmin' 'round. Johnny Reb's gonna think he knocked over a beehive if he tries attackin' that place."

Jack, who kept fading in and out of consciousness,

could only grunt in reply, but Boone gave a rousing bark of approval. A nearby soldier hearing Keener's assessment said, "Jess ahead is Malvern Hill. I heared one o' the officers say that's where Little Mac's makin' his last stand."

The Bucktails emerged from the woods and stomped up an open slope, that Keener judged to be about a half-mile wide, toward the Union defenses above them. Up they climbed into the first tier of earthworks where they were told to spread out and get their rifles ready. Joe lay Swift gently down and unbuttoned his heavy wool coat to make him more comfortable. He fanned the lad with his hat until Jack sat up and moaned, "W-W-Where are we?"

"Safe at last, laddie, in a hillside fort that no Reb's gonna breach."

"Praise the Lord."

"And get those guns primed!" snapped a testy lieutenant through his dirty moustache.

Joe took his position in the line behind the thick mound of dirt thrown up for the troops' protection. Checking his watch, he saw that it was just after noon. He stared down the naked slope until his eyes began swimming from the heat. Finally, he slumped forward in an exhausted slumber.

Keener was jarred awake by the rumble of cannon thunder. Below him the first wave of Rebs was just breaking from the protection of the trees to charge headlong toward him. Their defiant cries seemed very far away and were soon drowned out by the bellowing big guns. The batteries beside and above Joe banged again and again to rain down a fearful storm of canister and case shot that annihilated all it fell upon. In a matter of minutes, the attacking force was reduced to a few shocked survivors. Keener almost felt sorry for the Rebs who stumbled back the way they came only to be further pummeled by the heavy guns of Union riverboats patrolling the James. These shells shook the woods, blowing down limbs and creating reeking craters in the shattered earth.

A great cheer rose from the Union defenses followed by a long silence that allowed Keener and his worn-out mates to lapse into another dead slumber. The boom of Reb cannons shook them awake an hour later. This barrage was ineffective and lasted only a few minutes before the horrible, accurate fire of Federal siege guns came hurtling down from the sky. The enemy field pieces were smoking, shattered shards of twisted metal after but two such barrages.

In awe of the dreadful devastation, Joe stared down the slope to find fresh Confederate forces charging recklessly up the incline of death. They fired as they came, and puny puffs of smoke rose from their muskets. The mosquito whine of Reb bullets was soon replaced by the thunderous concussion of two hundred heavy cannons barking in unison. Canister and case shot again swept the slope, mowing down men with bloody thoroughness. As each charge was repulsed, another pushed forward only to be annihilated. The Union cannon crews worked with such machine-like precision that Joe muttered numbly to Jack, "Our boys is as calm as if they was takin' target practice."

"How kin a general called the Gray Fox keep sendin' his men ta be slaughtered like that? I can't watch no more," cried the lad, covering his eyes with his grimy hands.

Boone, though, seemed to be enjoying the artillery's prowess. After he got used to the continuous racket, the dog ran back and forth across the top of the breastwork. Yapping defiantly at the distant Rebs, he pranced and danced and watched the explosions below. Only when his tail got nipped by a bullet, did he dive to safety behind the earthen wall.

The Rebels continued to send assault after assault until the slope was so thick with corpses that the succeeding waves of gray soldiers could hardly step over them. Mercifully, darkness fell to end the carnage, and Keener mumbled, "A lot o' brave fellas died down there. Gotta admire 'em even if they is the enemy."

"I'm jess glad the tables wasn't turned," sighed Swift. "I don't know what I'd do if I was asked ta charge inta such fearful fire."

"You'd do as you was ordered like the rest o' us. After all the hard fightin' you done, I reckon you've got jess as much grit as any o' these other fellas."

"Thanks, Joe!" grinned Jack, boxing his friend on the arm. "I'm glad ya got so much confidence in me."

It hadn't been dark long before word passed down the line that the Union Army was to retreat from their hilltop stronghold. Keener was stunned by the news. He was about to vent his frustration when he heard General Phil Kearney growl, "After such a great victory, how can we fall back? I say to you all, such an order can only be prompted by cowardice or treason."

The Bucktails were rousted into formation by their dirty mustached lieutenant and set out on yet another night march. They stole down the eastern slope of Malvern Hill and cut around its base to the road leading to Harrison's Landing. Powder smoke still hung in the air, helping to mask their movement. With little fear of harassment from the battered Rebs, fires had been lit along the road to make sure the retreating troops didn't lose their way. Jack and Joe stumbled along with their eyelids heavy as lead. Their entire bodies were numb, and only the timely barking of Boone kept them from falling asleep on their feet.

Just before dawn a heavy downpour pummeled the men and turned the road into a sea of squishy mud. "Fall out!" ordered their lieutenant. "Make fer them woods!"

The Bucktails broke for the shelter of an oak grove where they scrambled to erect shebangs of limbs and canvas. Despite their shelters, they soon were drenched by wind-blown rain that stung exposed skin. After the deluge had ended, a horde of mosquitoes and biting flies descended to harry the soldiers. Finally, the swatting Jack howled, "I thought ya said we'd be safe once we reached Malvern Hill. If this is safe, I'd like ta know what you'd call bein' in danger."

"Well, laddie, at least there ain't no Reb Minie balls nippin' at yer rear er threatenin' ta knock yer head off. Bobbie Lee's got his own wounds ta lick now, so I reckon we ain't got much ta worry 'bout 'til we gits sent someplace even more miser'ble than this dang mud hole they calls the Peninsula."

Reenactor Gary Gilmore demonstrates the firing of a Civil War mortar. Mortars were used for crushing fortifications or setting them on fire. The mortar projectile was fired high in the air. Its weight rather than its velocity produced damage to what it fell on.

CHAPTER TWELVE:
RESTING AND REFITTING

The flies and mosquitoes soon drove the Bucktails from their makeshift camp in the oak grove. Forgetting their weariness, they scrambled into marching formation and slogged off down the road to Harrison's Landing. They hadn't marched far before Keener spotted the Union bivouac stretched out on a low plain beside the James River. At first glance, it looked to be ideally suited for McClellan's new base. A hill bristling with cannon defended its front, while gunboats steamed constantly past on the river beyond. It wasn't until a horrible stench wafted from the landing that Joe suspected the worst. "What in tarnation is that stink?" he grumbled. "This place reeks like a thousand latrines dug side-by-side!"

"Maybe it's yer breath backin' up on ya," laughed Jack.

"Ha! Ha! Ya won't think it's so funny when ya gotta eat yer meals breathin' that in!"

"It's jess 'bout suppertime. That probably is the meals!"

As the Bucktails splashed into camp, a familiar figure on a white horse came galloping up to greet them. Noting the officer's bulging eyes, pointy nose, and bushy, black beard, Joe shouted, "It's Colonel McNeil, boys, back from his bout with the fever. Let's give 'im a cheer!"

A ragged yell rose from the little band of tattered survivors, and the colonel suddenly burst into tears. When the haggard men marched nearer, he croaked, "My God! Where are my Bucktails? Would that I had died with them."

McNeil led his battered regiment to their assigned portion of camp, and the soldiers busied themselves erecting tents and getting cook fires started. Afterward, the men were marched down to the landing where liberal rations were distributed to them from a makeshift warehouse thrown up near a long wharf.

"Look at all that hardtack," whistled Jack, pointing to the multitude of wooden boxes stacked in a corner behind the quartermaster's helpers who handed out their provisions.

"And you're to get a full week's supply," winked a jolly clerk. "Don't come back at least until tomorrow for some more."

"Now, I know where them cattle went that we follered on the march," chuckled Keener. "Look at all the boiled beef they's givin' us. That should turn us scarecrows back inta men in no time."

The Bucktails returned to their bivouac and were excused from duty for three full days to rest and recuperate. Most of the time Jack and Joe spent snoring in their tent oblivious to the flies and mosquitoes and stench of the camp. On the evening of the third night, Swift discovered that he was crawling with lice. "I reckon it's time ta wash this here uniform," he said, scratching himself vigorously.

"That ain't a good idea," replied Keener, digging at his own vermin population.

"Why not?"

"'Cause the only thing holdin' these here clothes tagether is the dirt."

Colonel McNeil had also noticed the sorry condition of their uniforms. The next day he marched his Bucktails to a different wharf to be issued new sack coats and pants.

"I need a new kepi cap, too," chimed Jack when he received his clothes. "Mine got blowed off my head in one o' them there battles. We fought so many that they all kinda blur tagether."

"Whatcha gonna do fer a deer tail?" asked Keener.

"Some o' the other fellas sent home fer some. Once they a-rrive, I reckon I kin borrow er buy one."

"Jess make sure they don't stick ya with a doe tail," warned Joe.

"How kin ya tell the difference?"

"By the smell!" cackled Keener.

"I-I-I don't understand."

"How old did ya say ya was?"

"Thirteen."

"When ya gits ta runnin' with gals, Jack, you'll understand. Soon enough!"

The Bucktails' days of lazing about camp ended abruptly when General Seymour paid them a visit one morning. Major Stone had recovered from his hand wound and engaged in a lively conversation with the general.

"I need a bridge built over that creek flowing into the James over yonder," said the general, "but the engineers said it would take several days to finish AFTER they got the material. I can't wait that long! Herring Creek is disrupting communications between the wings of our army. That could spell disaster."

"Sir, most of our boys are lumbermen," replied Stone. "I'll bet they could do the job in half that time and with what's on hand."

"But that stream is a good four hundred feet wide and in places ten feet deep."

"No problem, General Seymour. Just leave it to us Bucktails. We'll get right at it!"

With no officers experienced in logging still left in the depleted ranks, Joe Keener was put in charge of the work party. The men were issued double-bladed axes and then followed Joe off into the woods north of camp. Keener's trained eye chose only the best timber that the men fell with smooth, powerful stokes. Jack and the other unskilled soldiers were given the job of trimming off the branches. By nightfall they had enough rough-hewn lumber to begin building.

While Jack and his crew held torches, the other Bucktails waded into Herring Creek to erect the bridge pilings. Their splashing and hammering echoed through the night. Spurred on by Keener's curse-laden instructions, the practiced loggers did not rest until dawn revealed to General

Seymour's surprised eyes a completed structure that even included a hand rail.

"Well done!" blustered the general as the weary Bucktails filed past on their way back to camp. "Take the rest of today off. If there's ever anything I can do for you boys, be sure to let me know."

"How 'bout getting us some oil o' gladness?" replied Keener with a grin.

"No, I wouldn't want you falling off that bridge you just built," laughed Seymour. "Nice try, anyway, Private."

With the Rebs no longer harassing them, the Bucktails turned to battling other foes. The muddy flats on which they were camped bred particularly vicious brands of flies and mosquitoes. The only effective way they found to discourage this scourge of insects was to eat their meals around very smoky fires. One night as they were choking on the smoke, Jack coughed, "I heared tell that the Indians coated theirselves with bear grease an' mud ta dis-courage bitin' bugs."

"Yeah, but that re-pellent worked too good fer them savages," winked Joe.

"What do ya mean?"

"Why, that bear grease kept the squaws away from 'em, too, an' that's why some tribes done vanished from the face o' this here earth!"

"Joe, you must be spendin' too much time at the latrine. That's gotta be where ya come up with them stories o' yers."

"You're right. That bad-tastin' canal water we's been forced ta drink has given me a wicked case o' the Virginy Quickstep. I gotta find me a clear runnin' spring mighty soon er there won't be e-nough o' me left ta hike ta the latrine."

"Some farmers been sellin' tomatoes, cabbages, an' such 'round camp. Soon as our regiment gits paid ag'in, I'll git us some. All that boiled beef can't be helpin' ya none, neither."

"Yeah, I thought I been bellowin' a sight more than usual. I musta scared Boone outta ten years o' his life with all the noise I been makin'."

"But most dogs only live ten years."

"Then, I best lay off that beef!"

A couple days later Jack and Joe were wandering around camp when they saw Major Stone in his tent packing his gear. Clearing his throat, Keener said, "Excuse me, sir, I hope that wounded hand o' yers ain't sendin' ya home. We'd be mighty sorry ta lose ya after how ya kept our fat from the fire durin' all them battles we jess fought."

"Oh, I'm not retiring from the army, Private Keener. I'm being sent home to recruit some new Bucktails."

"Hallelujah, sir! Our ranks is thinner than a Reb's britches."

"Same old Keener!" laughed Stone. "Unfortunately, it looks like I won't be sending many troops back to help you boys. There's talk of me enlisting a new regiment. Colonel McNeil's the one who suggested it. He's sending Captain Wister with me to help out. We might end up with a whole brigade of new sharpshooters."

"Would them outfits also be called 'Bucktails'?" asked Jack shyly.

"Certainly, soldier."

"Excuse me fer sayin' so, sir, but that's bogus!" blurted Keener.

"Not with me training them," replied Stone stiffly. "I know that many old veterans like you won't be too happy about sharing the Bucktail symbol. With the reputation you've won by hard fighting and great marksmanship, I can't blame you. Because of that reputation, so many civilians will want to become Bucktails that we'll be forced to start more regiments of valuable skirmishers."

"Well, good luck, sir," replied Jack, dragging the fuming Keener away before he said something else to offend Stone. "I hope yer hand don't give ya no more trouble."

Before Keener and Swift could share the major's news with the regiment, Colonel McNeil emerged from a neighboring tent and ordered the Bucktails to get their muskets and fall in.

"The dang Rebs musta brung up a new army," muttered Joe.

"Hey, I even pre-fers fightin' over stayin' in this here camp," replied Swift. "I'm ready ta go anyplace that ain't stunk up with mud."

Instead of taking the road out of camp like they expected, the Bucktails joined a long line of soldiers outside the ordnance warehouse. The line was slow moving and stretched a good quarter mile. The afternoon sun was scorching, and Joe watched many soldiers wither and faint from the oppressive heat of it. Grumbling became contagious until the first to enter the building ahead returned brandishing new rifles. While Keener watched their celebration, he said, "I'll bet we gits Sharps. We's jess as good marksmen as them Berdan boys, an' they got 'em."

"Wouldn't that be somethin'!" jabbered Jack. "Jess think how fast we could rattle off catridges if we got us breechloaders."

"An' how many Reb charges we could stop. Gettin' them guns would be like triplin' the size o' our regiment."

"They's accurate, too!" exclaimed Swift. "I seen a Berdan Colonel pick off a Reb at 600 yards with his Sharps. After he made that offhand shot, the officer said he wouldn't take a hundred dollars fer his gun."

"Yeah," replied Joe, "the only ones that has anything bad ta say 'bout them Sharps is the Rebs."

After standing in the baking sun for four hours, the Bucktails ducked inside the dark ordnance warehouse. A clerk collected their Springfield and Enfield muskets as they entered the door. Next, they were herded to a corner lit only by a sputtering oil lamp. Squinting in disbelief, the riflemen saw the quartermaster open a crate and begin unloading Harper's Ferry muskets to issue them. Keener took one look at the new guns and snarled, "We couldn't hit the stinkin' James River with them smoothbores! W-W-Why, they ain't half as good as the rifles we jess give ya. We wants Sharps!"

"Yeah!" echoed the Bucktails around him. "An' not the carbines neither!"

"Sharps! Sharps! Sharps!" chanted the rest of the men until the entire building echoed with the belligerent roar of their voices.

The quartermaster swallowed his Adam's apple several times before muttering, "S-S-Sorry, fellas. This is the ordnance ordered for you. . . by General--"

"Then we don't want any guns!" roared Colonel McNeil, his face purple with rage. "Come on, Bucktails!"

With their colonel leading the way, the regiment wheeled and furiously stomped out of the warehouse. As they marched grimly past the wharf, Joe Keener saw some familiar looking crates being unloaded from a steamer. Upon spotting them, he said, "Excuse me, Colonel McNeil, but ain't them guns bein' un-loaded from yonder supply ship?"

"Yes, indeed," grinned McNeil. "We should inspect them a bit closer. Fall out, men. Let's see what we have here."

Joe Keener read the label stamped on the end of each crate. After sifting through a whole stack of Enfield boxes, his ruddy face cracked into a huge grin. Picking up a crowbar, he ripped open a crate from a different stack. He reached a huge paw inside and unearthed a grease packed Sharps, which he handed to his colonel. One-by-one he distributed the rest of the guns in the crate and turned to rip open another box. When he had supplied half the regiment, a burly bosun's mate yelled from the ship's railing above him, "What are you apes doing down there?"

"Is that any way to address a U.S. Colonel?" growled McNeil in reply. "The quartermaster didn't have Sharps in the warehouse to supply us, so we're getting our weapons here. Of course, we could put all the guns back and have you and your men break your backs lugging them all the way over there if you'd prefer."

"No, sir! You go right ahead and help yourselves."

The Bucktails returned jubilantly to camp cradling their new Sharps. They spent the rest of the afternoon cleaning the excess grease from the barrels. They had just got their guns ready for firing when a huffy band of Berdan Sharpshooters stomped up the company street wearing dark scowls. The Berdan colonel marched straight to Colonel McNeil's headquarters, and Keener heard him rumble, "Do you know, sir, that your Bucktails appropriated our guns?"

"And what guns are those?"

"You know darn well--the Sharps!"

"Well, I don't recall ever seeing your name on them anywhere."

"Just the same, those Sharps belong to us. We came to collect them!"

"How do you propose to do that?" asked McNeil with a menacing stare.

"I-I-I'll get orders," blustered the Berdan colonel. "And have you court-martialed!"

The green uniformed officer continued to threaten until General Seymour, passing over the Herring Creek Bridge, hastened into camp.

"So you're behind all this confounded noise," said Seymour, striding between the two bristling colonels. "What's going on here?"

"These Bucktails stole our new rifles!" accused the Berdan officer.

"You mean from your bivouac?"

"No! They swiped our Sharps before we got them."

"Swiped them?"

"Yes, sir! Took them right off the dock."

"Well, Colonel, if you never got them in the first place, how can you say they're yours?"

"Um. . . because the quartermaster said our shipment of guns was on the steamer."

"I thought you said the Bucktails took the Sharps off the dock? If your guns were still on the steamer, then someone else must have appropriated them. I suggest you march that regiment of yours back to camp and cool off. If your guns were misplaced on the ship, you'll just have to wait for others to arrive."

"But, sir!" protested the Berdan colonel.

"That's enough! You have your orders."

"Yes, sir. Okay, men, you heard the general. Move out."

After the green uniformed riflemen had filed dejectedly away, General Seymour said to McNeil with a wink, "All that hard work your boys did on the bridge is appreciated, Colonel. I know they will work equally hard to defeat the Rebs with those new breechloaders of theirs."

"Thank you, sir. For everything."

Reenactor Robert Burns prepares himself a meal while relaxing in camp.

CHAPTER THIRTEEN:
A JOYFUL REUNION

"Hey, Jack, ain't them yer two brothers comin'?" asked Joe Keener pointing down the Bucktail company street.

Squinting from the bright August morning sun, Swift stared off toward the James River to find a troop of men marching slowly toward him. Their gait was halting, almost confused, as they tramped closer. The soldiers' new uniforms hung loosely on their bony frames. Their bucktailed hats were oversized and slid well down onto their ears. Their countenances, though familiar, wore a wizened look. The weariness visible in every eye was haunting. Finally, Jack picked two oval-faced lads from the ranks and leaped up to screech excitedly, "Zack! Jude! Welcome back!"

The next instant, the lad rushed to throw his arms around his siblings, and the three Swifts broke into an impromptu dance loosely resembling a jig. Boone loped to join them and added his yelps to the joyful reunion. Joe, meanwhile, went to shake hands with Sergeant Blett and Enos Conklin, who returned as gaunt caricatures of their former selves.

"Ain't it 'bout time fer lunch?" asked Conklin by way of greeting.

"Looks like you boys missed more 'n' a few meals, sure as shootin'," replied Keener. "Set right down by the fire pit, an' I'll heat up some boiled beef fer ya. That's 'bout all we's got 'cept fer a watermelon I jess bought fer $1.25 from a greedy tidewater farmer. I'll fetch that, too."

The returned Bucktails rushed to devour the food that Keener prepared for them. Jack and Joe watched in amazement as the riflemen crammed beef in their mouths and swallowed it half-chewed. They ate the watermelon, seeds and all, and looked around for more after it was gone.

"You boys sure put away them vittles," chuckled Keener. "Ya best check an' see that ya didn't eat none o' yer fingers by mistake."

"We're almost as hungry for news," replied Daniel Blett. "We learned nothing of the war while being held prisoner in Richmond."

"Us boys fought four battles in six days durin' the retreat ta this stinkin' mud hole," sighed Joe, "but I'd rather hear 'bout what happened ta Company K."

"Yeah," said Jack, sitting down between his brothers. "I've been worried as a cat dropped down a well 'bout ya. I can't wait no more ta hear that story o' yers!"

"The last time we saw you," began Daniel, "you and Joe left with Lieutenant Patton to find Major Stone. Soon after that, the distant sound of gunfire became a lot louder. Finally, Captain Irvin decided we better retreat, official orders or not. He formed us up on the road, and we backtracked toward Meadow Bridge."

"By then, there was Rebs swarmin' all 'round us, an' we was in a real fix!" exclaimed Zack, wiping the watermelon juice off his chin with his coat sleeve.

"That's right," explained Blett. "We hadn't gone far before we heard a Confederate officer tell his men to watch who they shot at because their whole army was coming down the Chickahominy, advancing along the riverbank. Then we tried to break through by a different route leading to the junction of the three roads defended by Company B."

"That was a stirred up bee's nest, too," grumbled Jude Swift. "That left us with no choice but ta take ta the swamp."

"Oh, you poor fella!" cried Jack, giving Jude a hug. "Was there snakes there?"

"You bet!" muttered Conklin. "I had a real tussle with a water moccasin that swam right fer my leg. I had ta choke it ta death, with it twistin' and squirmin' ta bite me. Didn't dare shoot, er the whole dang Reb army woulda been down on us."

"We had ta keep still most o' the time, fer sure," continued Jude, "'cause there was a steady line o' Rebs goin' by 'til dark. Sometimes they was only a hundred yards away. We was lucky they didn't spot us."

"We laid low all night, an' the next day we heared a terrible battle ta the east back at the Beaver Dam Creek line we wanted ta reach," said Zack. "Everyone o' us fellas was sure you boys would whip them Rebs an' drive 'em back ta Richmond, so we could es-cape."

"We give 'em what-for," grinned Joe. "Us Pennsylvania Reserves held off most o' Bobbie Lee's army all by ourselves. If old Stonewall hadn't flanked us, we might be pullin' out Jeff Davis' beard by the handfuls right now."

"We didn't realize how cut off we were," sighed Daniel grimly, "until that night. Scouts were sent out in every direction, and they all came back to report the whole line of the road between us and safety was lit up with enemy campfires."

"After that, the firin' got farther an' farther away," grunted Jude. "We figgered the Rebs was winnin' but didn't know no details 'til a Reb de-serter by the name o' John Robb was captured runnin' through the swamp. John told us our boys was retreatin' an' wanted ta lead us north back ta Fredericksburg where he was from. We was too stubborn ta listen. We figgered by workin' our way through the swamps at night, we could outfox the Rebs an' join back up with ya. Our own pride done us in, fer sure."

"As the Good Book says, 'Pride goeth before destruction, and an haughty spirit before a fall,'" quoted Daniel sadly.

"Our growlin' bellies interfered some with our thinkin', too," added Enos. "We hadn't ate in five days by then."

"One night Captain Irvin and his officers went out to reconnoiter the countryside," continued Blett. "They left me in charge of the men. As soon as Irvin left, the others said they wanted to surrender. I tried to talk them out of it, but they wouldn't listen."

"That was our bellies talkin' again," reasoned Conklin. "Anyhow, the captain returned before we could give ourselves up. He held a council an' per-suaded us ta make one more try ta escape. If we reached the Mechanicsville Road, Irvin said, we'd fight our way through. If the Rebs spotted us sooner, we'd give up."

"We sure picked a dandy night fer our es-cape," said Jude sarcastically. "We'd only gone a little way when a miser'ble thunderstorm pelted us. We jess made it ta a Reb railroad an' had ta cross the open grade where sentries was posted. We was all scared that the flashes o' lightnin' would come jess when one o' the fellas was dashin' 'cross the tracks, an' he'd be seen by the Rebs. Captain Irvin got over first. He signaled fer the rest o' us ta foller one at a time. 'Bout half had made it when we hears a cannon boom off Richmond way an' another boom on our side o' the river. Pretty soon this here train comes clatterin' out o' the dark, its headlight shinin' right where we'd been crossin'. We hunkered in the brush at the side o' the grade. The engine was so close, I could see the weasely face o' the dang engineer. He stopped his engine right opposite us an' yelled fer the sentries. We thought we was gonners, fer sure. After they'd yammered back an' forth awhile, the train ag'in creaked inta motion, an' the guards went back ta their posts. Some o' the boys had ta clean out their drawers after such a close call. We all got away safe, jess the same."

"I'll bet you was shakin' like Boone crappin' a peach stone!" whistled Joe, giving the hound a friendly pat on the head.

"We sure were," affirmed Sergeant Blett. "And the worst of it wasn't over by a long shot!"

"Well, what happened then?" asked Jack, his eyes widening in anticipation.

"After gettin' lost in the dark a coupla times an' soaked by buckets o' rain," replied Enos, "the next mornin' we come out 'tween Mechanicsville an' the river. There was a whole passel o' Rebs camped on a hill jess above us, so we didn't dare stay where we was. Ta git away, we had ta cross an open place in the swamp a good hundred yards wide. Like at the railroad, one-by-one we run across it. We figgered we was safe when everybody made it 'cept fer Zack an' another fella, who was both mighty fast. Jess as Zack streaked from the bushes, a dang straggler seen 'im an' give a yell."

"I still don't know how he seen me," interrupted Zack. "I was movin' faster 'n' a downhill locomotive!"

"Our bacon was fried then, just the same," concluded Blett. "We were only five miles from Richmond and totally surrounded by the enemy. We hadn't eaten in six days and were worn out from our all-night hike. The poor Bucktail who waved his handkerchief for a white flag bawled like a baby."

"Didn't the Rebs give ya no rations when they saw how bad off ya was?" asked Joe, snuggling closer to Boone.

"Not 'til we was marched all the way ta Richmond," grumbled Conklin. "Then, all they give us was a bushel o' soda crackers!"

"Yeah, the Rebs was too hard up ta feed us prisoners much," added Jude, "but I didn't let it bother me none. After livin' with our pap, there weren't too much they was gonna do ta hurt me."

"They didn't whip us none, anyhow," added Zack, rubbing the scar on his face. "They jess starved us an' such an' stuck us in the basement of an old tobaccy warehouse. Boy, was it hot down there! An' the lice an' maggots was crawlin' thick."

"It was the rats that gave me fits," shuddered Sergeant Blett. "Every night the high tide coming up the river pushed them into the building in droves. The squeak of those rats drove me crazy! I didn't dare sleep just thinking about them crawling on me."

"I seen you fight at Dranesville, Sergeant," said Jude. "You're a mighty brave fella. What is it 'bout rats that turns ya to jelly like that?"

"When Mary Ellen, my first-born, came along, my dear

wife and I thought it best to keep her crib in the kitchen near the stove where she would stay nice and warm. One night we heard her squalling. I pulled on my boots and ran down the hall to find a huge rat in bed with her. It had just poised itself to gnaw on my darling baby's nose. When I grabbed the filthy rodent, it bit me hard on the thumb. I flew into a rage and squeezed it until its eyeballs popped out of its head. Then, I flung it on the floor and stomped it until there was nothing left but a bloody spot beneath my boots! The bite got infected, and I got mighty sick. I was out of my head for days. The whole time I kept screaming for my wife to gets the rats off me. . . ."

"After hearin' that, I'm not gonna sleep tonight," said Jack, wincing.

"Well, at least ya got away from them rats when they transferred us ta Belle Island," reminded Zack.

"That weren't no picnic neither," grumbled Enos. "The island weren't more 'n' six acres, an' they penned us up there like cattle. There was an earth wall an' a ditch surroundin' the whole place. The lucky fellas had Sibley tents full o' holes ta sleep in. The rest o' us jess lived outdoors. There was twelve regiments o' men packed in there, too, an' never e-nough food."

"We had a really good escape plan worked out," reminisced Blett, "but an inmate ratted on us. The very day we were to carry out our plan, cannons were wheeled into position on two sides of Belle Island and the guard doubled. Later, we found out that a fellow from the Second Massachusetts was the tattler. He had been born in the South and sold us out for special privileges."

"Don't ya remember how he come inta camp all inno-cent like after he squealed?" asked Jude with a sneer. "We fell on him right quick an' woulda done 'im in if the guards hadn't come ta his rescue. That was the last we seen o' that snitch."

"But, hey, ya all survived!" whooped Jack. "I'm so glad ya got ex-changed! I'll bet the Rebs de-manded a general in return fer so many sharpshootin' Bucktails."

"An' we's double glad ta see you!" shouted Zack, giving his brother another hug.

"Guess what?"

"What's that, Jack?" asked Jude, cuffing his brother playfully on the head.

"While you was away, I learned ta write my FULL name."

"Oh, Pap would be so proud!" mocked Jude.

"I figgered that dog ya picked up would have a better chance o' writin' than you," teased Zack.

"Joe learned me. An' he's a dang good teacher, too!"

"Keener, I always suspected you were a smart fellow although you tried your darnedest to hide it," kidded Daniel. "With the brains you have, why on God's green earth do you spend so much time drinking and clowning around?"

"I never took much serious in my en-tire life. My pappy run a sawmill an' wanted me ta go inta business with 'im. That's why he sent me ta school where they tried crammin' my head with book learnin'. But I was always spendin' too much time pullin' gals' hair an' droppin' polliwogs down their dresses ta pay school much mind. When I outgrowed them games, I met up with Hosea Curtis an' grad-uated ta the tavern. Soon, I was cuttin' the timber that ended up at Pappy's mill. He was mighty disappointed when I left fer the loggin' camp but told me the door was always open if I changed my mind 'bout bein' his partner."

"Well, Joe, maybe you'll make yer mark in the army with that there education o' yers," said Zack. "They's always lookin' fer good sergeants an' such."

"An' he'd make a good one, too!" exclaimed Jack. "You shoulda seen how he got the boys ta build yonder bridge over Herring Creek."

"I'd put in a good word for you if you wanted pro-moted," assured Sergeant Blett. "You're an experienced soldier now and should get some stripes for all your hard fighting."

"A sergeant? Not me! I'm jess interested in savin' my own bacon. I don't wanna worry 'bout nobody else."

"Then why did ya carry me all them miles durin' the retreat?" asked Jack. "I'da been a goner if ya hadn't."

"I didn't want yer dog ta git lonely is all," grinned Joe, rubbing Boone's floppy ears. "Hey, did you boys hear the joke 'bout the lousy general, the blind quartermaster, an' the cake o' lost soap?"

"Oh, no!" groaned Enos. "Not another dang story. Keener, you're completely hopeless!"

CHAPTER FOURTEEN:
BACK TO THE WAR

Captain Irvin returned to lead Company K by the middle of August. With a scowl etched on his boyish face, he trudged into camp with the other exchanged officers. The scraggly goatee that had become his trademark still lingered on the tip of his chin. The determination burning in his eyes remained undiminished by his incarceration.

Irvin searched unsuccessfully for his command until he saw Zack and Jack Swift throwing each other fly balls with a baseball made of wrapped rags. When the brothers spotted their captain, they rushed to slap him on the back until they were quietly reminded that wasn't the proper way to greet an officer.

"Sorry, sir," apologized Zack. "We was jess so happy ta see ya that we done fergot our manners."

"Apology accepted, Private Swift."

"Yeah, sorry, Captain," said the younger brother.

"I'm glad to see you survived the campaign, Jack."

"Thank ya, sir. We's been wonderin' what become o' ya."

"It took longer for us officers to get exchanged is all. The Confederates finally let us go at Aiken's Landing. You boys are dismissed. Go on with your practicing. Who knows when we'll be playing another game."

"Hopefully, the next one'll be in Curwensville," replied Zack with a wink.

Ed Irvin had little time to get settled in at Harrison's Landing, for the very next morning the Bucktails were assembled by Colonel McNeil and marched to the waiting steamer <u>Kingston</u>. As they filed aboard, Joe Keener said,

"Ain't it bully we's gettin' out o' this mud hole o' a camp!"

"Hey, at least here we had all we could eat," muttered Enos Conklin.

"An' the next place we's sent could be worse," grumbled Jude.

"I'm with Keener," said Sergeant Blett. "I'd rather be anywhere than in this stinking swamp hole."

"Anywhere but that Richmond tobaccy warehouse," chuckled Zack.

"I don't care where they send me," added Jack, stooping to pet the company mascot, "as long as Boone gits ta go along."

The Kingston emitted a long blast from its steam whistle and started down the James River estuary. The Bucktails lined the rail and cheered when they were underway. The day was sunny and the spirits high until they reached Old Point Comfort where the steamer suddenly hove to.

"Why's we stoppin' here?" asked Enos with a frown. "We had a nice breeze ta cool us when we was movin'. Now, we's gonna melt in this heat."

"We must be out of coal," replied Blett. "I believe this is a navy refueling station."

"Then why don't we go ashore?" said Joe with a suggestive grin. "There's gotta be someplace close by where we kin quench our hot thirsts."

"Or catch a Reb bullet," added Captain Irvin. "No one is going anywhere."

"But after all we's been through on this stinkin' Peninsula, ain't we en-titled ta a little fun?" whined Enos.

"Yes, but not until we've taken care of our business with the Rebels," said Irvin softly. "If you boys are hot, go lie down in the shade over on the port side."

"See. Boone's already over there," chortled Zack. "He's got more brains than all o' us boys put together."

"Then they oughta make him sergeant," observed Keener wryly.

The Kingston lay waiting for three days to receive its

load of coal. Finally, the steamer hoisted its anchor, churned out of Hampton Roads, and steered for Chesapeake Bay. With the weather remaining fair, the Bucktails lounged about the deck soaking up the rich sunshine.

"I really needed this time to relax," said Daniel Blett. "I can feel all the knots go out of my muscles."

"Now, if the knots would go out o' Keener's head, we'd be all set!" joshed Zack.

"But then all the fight would leave him, and we'd have to make him our chaplain," laughed Daniel.

"Hey, there's plenty o' fightin' priests par-tcipatin' in this here war," replied Keener seriously.

"Name one!" challenged Jude.

"How 'bout Billy Pendleton?"

"Who the heck is he?" asked Conklin.

"Only the general in charge o' Bobbie Lee's en-tire artillery corps."

"But I thought you said he was a priest," snickered Jack.

"He was be-fore the war. As soon as the bullets started flyin', he turned in his collar fer a captain's commission. He musta had God on his side, fer he quickly got ta be General Joe Johnston's chief o' artillery be-fore takin' over fer Lee. It's said that he was 'specially proud o' four six-pound brass cannon he once was in charge of. He said they spoke a powerful language, so he named 'em Matthew, Mark, Luke, an' John fer the Catholic Saints!"

"Joe, where do ya come up with these yarns?" groaned Jude.

"What do ya mean by yarns?" asked Joe with a hurt frown. "I done read 'bout Pendleton in a Reb newspaper that a fella brung ta Harrison's Landin'."

"Yeah, it was probably wrapped 'round a bottle o' tanglefoot," needled Zack.

"Hey, I heared that we's on our way ta help out General Pope's army," said Enos. "What's with that?"

"Our old nemesis Stonewall Jackson's on the loose again," replied Sergeant Blett. "Lee sent him to attack Pope, who's been put in charge of the army guarding Washington. Ever since the Battle of Cedar Mountain, Pope's been hounding the president for more troops."

"That's us!" exclaimed Jude. "The Bucktails is always the first ta see action, an' the last ta leave it."

"Well, if it's any comfort to you," smiled Blett, "the rest of McClellan's army can't stay holed up by the James too much longer. Every soldier Mr. Lincoln has is going to be needed once the Gray Fox follows Jackson north."

"That'll take the heat off Richmond, sure as shootin', an' pro-long this here war fer at least another dang year!" moaned Conklin. "Sergeant, don't ya miss bein' away from yer wife fer so long?"

"Yeah," replied Daniel soberly, "there's plenty of nights I can't think of anything else but Catherine. But in battle, I don't dare. . ."

"If ya miss her so much, why don't ya have her come visit? Don't ya know that there's been plenty o' wives done follered their husbands off ta war?"

"Really, Joe?" asked Jack with a curious smile.

"Fer example, I heared tell o' this Kady Brownell who tagged along with her husband ta Bull Run after he en-listed. Durin' the battle, she took the place o' the Sixth Regiment's flag bearer when he stopped a bullet. She then pro-ceeded ta carry that there banner 'til she got wounded. Old Ambrose Burnside called her 'Child o' the Regiment' fer her bravery."

"Dang!" exclaimed Jack. "I wouldn't want no woman hangin' 'round the Bucktails like that."

"Why not?" asked Enos.

"'Cause she'd probably try motherin' me an' treat me like a little kid. After what I jess seen, that part o' me died on the Peninsula."

"That's why you should want a woman around," said Blett quietly. "A woman's love is what keeps us from growing too fond of war and the killing that goes with it."

"Gee, an' here I thought it was oil o' gladness that done that," chortled Joe.

The <u>Kingston</u> continued to steam steadily up Chesapeake Bay for the next three days. On the fourth morning, Keener was wakened by sailors scurrying past him on the deck. Rolling out of his blanket, he gazed over the rail to see the steamer heading for a landing at the mouth of a distant stream.

"That would be Aquia Creek," said Daniel Blett, yawning beside him.

"Then we's headed back ta Falmouth," replied Joe.

"Yeah, that would be the quickest route to join up with Pope."

"I jess wish we'd git back tagether with Kane's Bucktails," sighed Enos Conklin. "It'd be a real comfort ta be part o' a full regiment ag'in instead o' this skeleton crew."

"I'm surprised I ain't heared back from my old pal, Hosea Curtis," said Joe. "I'd sure like ta know what become o' Companies C, G, H, an' I. They got ta be part o' Pope's army, so I reckon our re-union with 'em can't be too far off."

The Kingston glided up to the Aquia Creek landing amid the shouts of officers and the squeal of bosuns' pipes. The Bucktails were hustled onto shore and herded into the boxcars of a waiting train. The engine lurched into motion before all the riflemen were even seated. When Joe, Jack, Zack, and Sergeant Blett toppled on top of Jude and Enos, curses burst from every corner of the crowded car.

"Boy, they must be in an all-fired hurry ta git us boys killed," grumbled Enos, pushing the squirming Jack off his chest.

"At least they could wait an' let the Rebs do it," snarled Jude. "Get off me, Keener, ya big ape!"

The troop train chugged up a slight grade and through some rolling hill country. Joe tried to peep through the boxcar slats at the passing scenery, but all appeared blurry in the gloominess of the afternoon. It wasn't until dark that the Bucktails arrived at Falmouth. After ammunition was crammed into their hands by waiting members of the quartermaster's corps, they set off immediately on the march up the north bank of the Rappahannock River.

"Ain't we gonna git no rations?" complained Enos

111

when they got underway.

"Maybe there's some in the two wagons taggin' along behind us," said Jack hopefully as Boone seconded his opinion with a gruff bark.

"Nah, they was stuffed full o' hospital tents, medicine, an' such," grunted Jude. "I watched 'em git loaded."

"If we ain't fed soon, there's gonna be a lot o' sick fellas," puffed Conklin, wiping clammy sweat from his brow.

Hushed to silence by Captain Irvin, the troops tramped glumly along in the darkness. They had only marched a couple of miles when the rumble of thunder announced the approach of a storm that broke over them moments later. Rain fell in sheets, making the way slippery for the stumbling men. The officers had such difficulty seeing that they lost the way, and the column had to backtrack several times. Finally, in frustration, Colonel McNeil ordered the men to find shelter the best they could.

Drenched to the skin, Keener was shivering too hard to fall asleep. He couldn't see two feet in any direction and only knew the location of his comrades from the chattering of their teeth. After what seemed like forever, the first light of dawn filtered through the trees. The storm finally abated, and the sun rose like a ball of fire from behind them.

"Get in line, men," ordered Colonel McNeil in a hoarse whisper. "We must reach Kelley's Ford and cross the river before the Rebs find us."

The Bucktails fell in and marched woodenly forward. The farther they tramped up the sloppy roads, the hotter the day became. By noon, the sweltering sun took a serious toll on the stamina of the soldiers. All around him, Keener watched his squad's faces grow pasty with sick sweat. Their tongues swelled with thirst, and many dropped to all fours to lap greedily at stagnant pools bordering the road. When Joe saw Jack Swift fall down near a puddle crusted over with scum, he yanked the lad rudely to his feet and hissed, "Even Boone's got the sense not to drink that slime, laddie. Do ya want yer guts ta rot out, er what?"

The First Rifles staggered along in the blazing sun until their eyes swam and their heads swirled dizzily. Finally, the whole regiment exhaled an exhausted groan and ground to a halt. The soldiers crawled and tottered for the nearest shade. Even Keener collapsed in a quivering heap, panting like a spent bruin.

"Get moving, men!" ordered Colonel McNeil from astride his tall, mud-splattered horse. "You're the fighting wildcats, and wildcats never surrender!"

"You heard the colonel!" wheezed Captain Irvin. "Get up!"

"Where's your pride, Bucktails?" challenged the colonel.

No matter how McNeil and Irvin threatened and cajoled the men, they remained breathing heavily in the shade. It wasn't long before General Meade galloped down the road to see what was causing the holdup. After running his goggle eyes over the spent soldiers, he rasped, "Bucktails, I can see how much you're suffering. If the lives of thousands of men didn't depend upon our timely arrival on General Pope's flank, I would order you to fall out and have a long rest. Unfortunately, war demands sacrifices of brave men like yourselves. Now, what do you wish to do, Bucktails? Lie here or go forward to the rescue of your comrades?"

"Go forward," croaked Keener.

"Go forward," repeated the other exhausted soldiers.

It wasn't unusual for wives to visit their husbands during the Civil War. Often, they came to nurse their spouses' wounds. Above, reenactor Colleen Nobles arrives at the Bucktail encampment to cook for her son Kyle and her huband Tom.

ROLE OF McNEIL'S BUCKTAILS
IN THE SECOND BATTLE OF BULL RUN

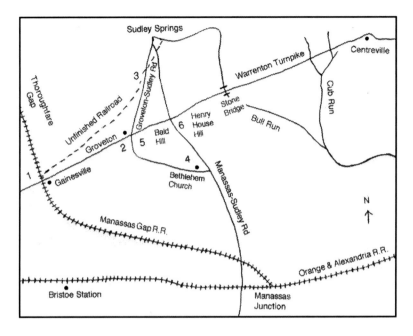

1. On the evening of August 27, 1862, the Bucktails bivouac near Gainesville, VA, where they see Manassas burning in the distance.
2. Just before noon on August 28 near Groveton, VA, a Rebel battery fires on the Bucktails as they march up the Warrenton Turnpike.
3. Captain Edward Irvin leads a Bucktail scouting party up the Groveton-Sudley Road. He is recalled before he makes contact with Stonewall Jackson's Rebels.
4. In the evening of August 28, the Bucktails are ordered to march to Manassas before being recalled to the Warrenton Turnpike.
5. On the morning of August 29, the Bucktails are engaged in hot fighting near Groveton. During the day, they participate in four unsuccessful Union attacks.
6. On August 30, 1862, the Bucktails help stop the final Rebel attack on Henry House Hill, allowing the beaten Union forces to escape across Bull Run.

CHAPTER FIFTEEN: MARCHING IN CIRCLES

"Pope's boys ain't in no danger," wheezed Jude when the Bucktails finally caught up with the Union Army at Rappahannock Station.

"An' here we done marched all afternoon fer nothin'," grumbled Conklin.

"Old Meade's a sly rascal, all right," gasped Keener. "I reckon he'da said anything ta keep us movin'."

"They call Meade 'Old Snappin' Turtle,'" cackled Zack wearily. "I'm jess glad we listened ta 'im when we did. I wouldn't want his tough, old jaws gnawin' on my be-hind, sure as shootin'."

The Bucktails fell in with the rear guard of Pope's army and, near exhaustion, stumbled on to Warrenton. Posted on the southern heights overlooking the town, the riflemen were dismissed from the ranks while other fresher units were assigned picket duty. Without bothering with supper, the men wrapped themselves in their blankets and immediately fell into an unconscious slumber.

Keener and his squad slept straight through reveille the next morning and had to be rousted awake by sleepy officers. They stumbled into rank for roll call and then were dismissed for breakfast. Badly needed rations were distributed to the spent men along with a shipment of mail.

"Hey, lookee here," grinned Joe after a soiled envelope was passed to him. "Old Hosea Curtis didn't fergit me, after all."

"Well, don't jess set there grinnin' like a baked possum," chided Jude. "Let's hear what the letter says."

"Okay. Okay. Keep yer britches on 'til I skims over it."

"Why ya gotta do that?" asked Jack, squirming with

anticipation.

"Probably his drinkin' buddy sent him a map o' the local taverns," needled Zack.

"It looks like Kane's boys jess been in another mighty tussle!" exclaimed Keener, ignoring Swift's jest.

"Are you going to keep us in suspense all morning?" growled Daniel Blett. "Read the darn letter, will you?"

"You sure is owly this mornin', Sergeant. Here's what Hosea wrote:

Howdy Joe,

J.E.B. Stuart's been up ta his old tricks. Last night us fellas was camped out at Catlett's Station guardin' Pope's baggage train when Stuart hit us in the middle o' a gol-dang thunderstorm. The rascal wanted ta burn the bridge over Cedar Creek, but he might as well o' tried burnin' the creek, the way it was pourin'! After them Rebs overrun our camp, we regrouped in the dark woods ta figger out what ta do. By then Stuart's horse soldiers was destroyin' Pope's wagons and tents.

With Colonel Kane leadin' us, we charged 'em. It was so dark, ya couldn't tell Yank from Reb 'cept when the guns er lightnin' flashed. We was mighty angry, let me tell ya, and hit 'em so hard they done run off with their tails 'tween their legs.

The next mornin' we learned that the Rebs got clean away with 300 prisoners, includin' our pickets. They also stoled money chests and papers tellin' the strength o' our troops. Stuart musta got a real chuckle outta robbin' General Pope's own uniform, horses, and equipment.

As usual, gol-dang Pope weren't in camp, er he mighta got captured hisself. The general's always braggin' 'bout how hard he works and that his saddle is his headquarters. Boone likes ta say that Pope's headquarters is where his hindquarters outta be!

Hope ta see ya soon.

Hosea"

117

"That Boone thinks he's quite the joker, don't he," snickered Zack.

"Thinks is 'bout it," groaned Keener.

"Jess wait 'til he learns we named our mascot after 'im," laughed Jack. "That'll put 'im in his place."

After the Bucktails joined Pope's army, their camp was shifted three times in as many days. Keener and his squad all wondered what was going on until Sergeant Blett rushed back to their bivouac one morning to growl, "Jackson's at it again, boys. I just heard that he marched around us, destroyed Bristoe Station, and cut our rail communications with Washington."

"Old Jack's like a rat ya can't trap," grumbled Enos Conklin.

"So let's hunt 'im down an' shoot 'im!" urged Jude.

"Go tell Pope that," replied Daniel. "He sure can't permit Jackson to operate in our rear."

"Then we best go pack our haversacks," grunted Joe. "Can't be long now be-fore we pulls out."

The words were barely out of Keener's mouth when the Bucktails were assembled into formation and began another march down the dusty Warrenton Turnpike. As they tramped along toward the rising, red sun, Joe noted the flags of the other Pennsylvania Reserve regiments that clogged the road ahead of him. Beyond the Reserves to the east was a long, blue line of the other units under the command of General McDowell.

"How many fellas do ya reckon we got in this here column?" asked Jack, gazing in wide-eyed admiration at the powerful force surging around him like a turbulent river.

"We must be 40,000 strong," replied Sergeant Blett. "That's more than enough Yanks to keep Stonewall from receiving reinforcements from the south. The trick is to be on the right road at the right time to block them."

"Where do ya think we're headin'?" asked Jude, after coughing to clear the dust from his throat.

"A sign back yonder said 'Gainesville,'" answered Joe. "If we stays on this here road, we'll e-ventually end up at

Bull Run."

"I'm jess glad I missed the first dang Manassas battle," grunted Enos Conklin.

"I'll bet Jackson is happy he fought there," said Daniel, "because that's where he earned his nickname. While other troops wavered, his men stood firm as a stone wall."

"An' he ain't 'bout ta buckle anytime soon, neither," muttered Enos.

The Bucktails marched in silence after Conklin's glum observation. The dust became increasingly worse with the heat of the morning, and many men wrapped moistened handkerchiefs around their mouths and noses to keep from choking. The soldiers stomped wearily on without a break until their eyes became blank pools of fatigue. The stiff movement of legs and feet created a cadence more suited to a funeral procession than an advancing army of battle-tested veterans. Even the Bucktails' mascot straggled along as though the life was being sucked out of him.

Finally, as the long shadows of dusk stretched out from the Bull Run Mountains, orders were given for the troops to fall out. The weary Bucktails stumbled into the fringe of the woods to build low fires made of pine twigs. Soon, coffee was boiling, and a soft glow rose from the bowls of lighted pipes. Conversations unraveled in the twilight and compensated greatly for the usual lack of rations.

"Hey, that night went mighty quick," yawned Jude, pointing to a redness that tinted the sky off to the southeast.

"That ain't the sun, you yahoo!" exclaimed Joe. "That's a mighty big fire!"

"And it's coming from the direction of the Union storehouse at Manassas," gasped Sergeant Blett.

"Looks like we ain't gonna git nothin' ta eat tomorrow neither," grumbled Enos, "with Old Jack's boys feastin' on our vittles."

"Well, at least we know where Stonewall is," said Zack, massaging Boone's weary legs.

"An' w-w-where we'll be h-h-headin' tomorrow," stuttered Jack nervously.

119

First light found the Bucktails formed up again on the Warrenton Turnpike. Progress was slow with the sleepy troops ahead stumbling along like a herd of uncooperative cattle. They hadn't gone far before the sun rose to bake the soldiers in their blue wool.

Just before noon Keener turned to check on Jack Swift, whose pace had slowed significantly. "How's ya doin'?" asked Joe, putting his arm around the lad's shoulders to steady him.

"Okay, I reckon. My tongue ain't lollin' on the ground like Boone's, anyhow."

"If ya needs me ta carry yer rifle er haversack fer a while, jess say so."

"Thanks, Joe. I'm still hoofin' it pretty good. Really."

Keener and his squad hadn't gone more than a few more steps when a distant boom was followed by the wicked swoosh of cannon shells. There was a mighty explosion up the road ahead and the screams of men blown skyward. When the next barrage hit a little closer, Jude Swift growled, "Leave it to Johnny Reb to throw some of his rotten balls in."

"An' mighty accurately, too!" exclaimed Enos.

In the next instant, Colonel McNeil came galloping back on his horse to bark, "Forward, Bucktails! Companies B, D, and K spread out in that open field there. The rest of you go reconnoiter the woods to the right. Skirmishers, forward!"

Keener and the other riflemen of Company K scrambled into the pasture to the left of the turnpike and spread out twenty feet apart. As they deployed, Joe could see the brigade behind him forming into a line of battle and a battery of cannon being unlimbered from their caissons. The Bucktails hadn't gone more than a quarter of the way across the field before the Union cannons began answering their Confederate counterparts with thunderous fire.

On the ridge ahead, the enemy gunners were scurrying about like gray ants furiously shooting and reloading their pieces. The Bucktails pushed steadily on blazing away with their Sharps at the puffs of smoke made by a thin line of Reb skirmishers in front of them. On just the third round of Union cannon fire, the Confederates suddenly melted into the woods, and all grew eerily quiet.

When Keener and his squad pushed to the top of the knoll, all they found were the impressions of cannon wheels and trampled places in the disturbed earth made by the evacuated artillery crews. Squinting in the noon sun, Joe stared off into the distance and then gave a low whistle. "Lookee there," he said, pointing to the woods below. "There's a big clump o' gray infantry down yonder. They coulda made it mighty hot fer us fellas had they stayed ta fight. What's Johnny Reb up ta, anyhow?"

"That's what you're going to find out," said Colonel McNeil, spurring his horse up the hill. "Captain Irvin, I want you to take your command up the Sudley Springs Road below us and see how many Rebels are actually there. That's probably Jackson's rear guard we ran into, but we'd better make sure."

"Yes, sir!" replied Irvin with a sharp salute. "Okay, men, let's get moving."

Captain Irvin led the three companies of Bucktails down a steep grade onto the Groveton-Sudley Road. They skidded down the last few feet of the incline and then spread into a thin skirmish line. Cautiously, the riflemen crept along peering into the ravines that bordered their path. With their Sharps held cocked and ready, they proceeded one silent step at a time.

Nervous sweat stood out on Joe Keener's forehead as he scanned the woods ahead. He was flanked by Sergeant Blett and Zack Swift. Jack, creeping along next to his brother, was accompanied by Boone. The hound was as vigilant as the men. He sniffed the ground and then the air and then the ground again. Suddenly, he broke growling for an adjacent thicket and returned herding an old, bent black man who had been cowering there.

"Look!" said Sergeant Blett. "Our mascot's caught a contraband."

"D-D-Don't shoot me, master," pleaded the slave. "Y-Y-You can call off your hound now. Please, master."

"Calm down," warned Captain Irvin, disturbed by the commotion. "Don't you see our blue coats? We aren't going to hurt you."

"Yeah, but that swarm of Rebs that passed by here was," replied the slave.

"What Rebs?" asked Irvin.

"Them foot and horse soldiers is what. A whole passel of 'em follered their retreatin' cannons just over yonder."

"How many Rebels were there?"

"More than this poor old head could count. They was plentiful as a swarm of bees, master."

"Well, come on, men," said the captain. "We better check out this fellow's story. Bring him along. We'll set him free once we get back to the main column."

Again, the Bucktails started toward Sudley Springs. They had only gone a short distance when Irvin hissed, "Take cover! There's some Reb cavalry just ahead."

The riflemen scrambled off the road and dove behind trees, rocks, and fallen logs. Upon reaching cover, they trained their Sharps on the distant cavalry in anticipation of the pounding of hooves that signaled an all-out assault by horse soldiers. Instead, the Rebs circled their mounts, held a brief counsel, and then fled in a whirlwind of shouts and dust.

"They musta seen our buck tails an' skedaddled," chortled Zack. "They didn't want no part o' marksmen like us."

"Or else they were under orders not to engage the enemy," said Sergeant Blett. "There's something funny going on here, for sure."

"I agree," seconded Captain Irvin. "I believe we won't have to go much farther to find out what those Rebs are up to. We'll soon know if they're Jackson's men or those sent to reinforce him."

Before the Bucktails could continue their reconnaissance, a dispatch rider galloped from behind them and reined in his horse next to Irvin. Scanning the message he was handed, the captain said with obvious disappointment, "Fall in, men. We've just been recalled by General Reynolds."

"Dang!" groaned Joe Keener. "An' jess when things was gettin' interestin'."

"Well, at least we won't have ta tangle with the Rebs all by ourselves," said Zack. "I've already seen all o' Richmond I care ta, if ya know what I mean."

The First Rifles stumbled into marching formation and retraced their steps to the Warrenton Turnpike. By the time they reached the rest of the Pennsylvania Reserves, their faces were flushed and their feet numb with fatigue. They fell in at the rear of the column and tramped along for two more hours in the blazing August afternoon heat. Now, the march led them down a side road to Manassas. Even Keener could barely keep pace by the time they reached a country church that loomed suddenly from the wayside.

"Hey, General Reynolds done marched us straight ta heaven," chortled Zack wearily when he saw the white steeple rising above the trees.

"Naw, that there's jess the Bethlehem Church," sighed Enos Conklin. "You're so tired, you're out o' yer head."

"Or seeing a mirage," chuckled Daniel Blett.

When the Bucktails arrived at a crossroads, they saw two signs tacked on a tree in plain view. On the upper sign was scrawled the word "Manassas" with an arrow pointing to the right. The lower one said "Sudley Springs" and pointed left. When the column followed the directions written on the second sign, Jude Swift moaned, "We jess come from there, fellas. Now, the dang brass has us marchin' in circles."

"Yeah, but listen," said Sergeant Blett, cocking his ear to the wind. "That's either cannon fire or a serious thunderstorm coming from where we were."

"That must be a battle, then, 'cause there ain't a cloud in the sky," muttered Conklin.

"At least there ain't time fer us ta march back there taday," sighed Joe, "an' I'm too tired ta worry 'bout tomorrow."

"Tomorrow will come soon enough," replied Daniel. "By then Stonewall Jackson's plans will be clear even to a nearsighted fellow like General Pope."

CHAPTER SIXTEEN:
SECOND BULL RUN

The next morning found the Bucktails dug in on a hill overlooking the Warrenton Turnpike near where they had been ambushed by the Reb battery the day before. Through the underbrush to his left, Keener could just discern blue troops massing for a dawn attack.

"Who are them boys?" whispered Joe. "They musta come up durin' the night."

"That's General Sigel's corps," replied Sergeant Blett. "Don't you see his flag?"

"The way General Reynolds has been ridin' back an' forth all mornin', I reckon we's gonna be guests at the Rebs' surprise party," chuckled Zack.

"Swift, I wouldn't be laughin' too loud," cautioned Enos. "Accordin' ta the telegraph grapevine, Jackson's got hisself a strong position over yonder in a railroad cut."

"But I thought Old Jack was at Manassas," said Jude.

"He was TWO days ago!" replied Conklin.

"But why ain't he there now?"

"Well, ya didn't think he'd stay an' let Pope catch 'im, did ya, Jude?"

"Yeah, it's reasonable he came here to allow his reinforcements to reach him," seconded Daniel.

"Then we'll jess have ta hit 'im hard before dang Longstreet a-rrives," Zack remarked.

As soon as it was fully light, Sigel's artillery erupted in a long, deafening barrage, and the Union attack was thrown forward. The Bucktails were deployed as skirmishers for the Pennsylvania Reserves on the extreme left flank of the advancing army. Keener and his squad moved cautiously through a thick wood but saw no sign of the enemy. By the hot musket fire to the right, Joe knew that Sigel's men had already made contact with Jackson's forces.

The Bucktails sneaked through the undergrowth until they came to the Warrenton Turnpike. General Meade rode up behind them leading a contingent of Reserves. Soon the pike was swarming with blue infantry that Old Snappin' Turtle barked at continually to hurry them into position. Joe chuckled as he watched the Fourth, Seventh, and Eighth regiments scurry for a ridge to the north with Cooper's battery close behind them. The Third Pennsylvania Reserves, meanwhile, were ordered to straddle the pike.

Finally, Meade rode up to McNeil and growled, "Take your men west toward Groveton, Colonel, until you make contact with the Rebs. If possible, stay there and protect our left flank."

"Yes, General. You can count on my Bucktails!"

The riflemen again spread into a skirmish line and moved purposefully up the pike. Everywhere were signs of the previous day's battle they had heard while on the march back from Bethlehem Church. Dead cavalry mounts littered the road along with shattered caissons. As Keener stepped over a horse that had been blown in half by a cannon shell, he muttered, "Maybe our walkin' in circles weren't that bad after all. I reckon we got outta here yesterday jess in time."

"Yeah," replied Sergeant Blett, "we were lucky the Rebs weren't in a fighting mood when we stumbled across them."

The Bucktails continued up the road until a little village could be seen in the distance. Here, McNeil ordered his men into battle formation, and the six companies moved in force toward a house just visible through the brush to the left of the pike.

"The Rebs can't be far off now," grunted Jude, peering warily into the undergrowth.

"They're so close I kin smell 'em," whispered Zack.

The riflemen took only a few more steps when the thunderous report of a hidden Reb battery shook the woods to the right. At the same instant, concealed gray sharpshooters let loose a volley from the thicket south of the road. As Keener dove for cover behind a splintered fence, he watched an exploding cannon shell catch Enos Conklin in its fury and blow his uniform into bloody rags. Conklin tumbled lifeless to the ground with surprise still caught on his face. A second volley of Reb bullets tore through the ranks before Joe remembered the Sharps clutched tightly in his huge paws.

Joe heard the Swift brothers' rifles spit a defiant reply before he, too, took aim at the Reb musket flashes winking from the thicket. Now, he saw that the enemy occupied the distant house, as well. Feeding linen cartridges into his Sharps, Keener soon was shooting three times faster than the musket toting Rebs. A gleam of determination grew stronger in his eyes each time he saw a gray shadow throw up its arms after he had squeezed off an accurate shot.

"Fix bayonets!" Keener heard Captain Irvin bark when the Reb musket fire began to slow. "Charge!"

In an instant Keener leaped to his feet and rushed with Company K headlong up the pike toward the Reb-occupied house. He was oblivious to the whining bullets whizzing past until he saw Zack grab his leg and sprawl headlong on his face. Swift lay writhing in pain, but Joe dared not stop to assist him. Instead, he bent forward at the waist and streaked straight for the Reb infested building. Using his huge shoulder for a battering ram, he smashed in the door, allowing his comrades to swarm in around him. His ears rang with rifle blasts inside the close quarters of the room. He bayoneted the first gray form he encountered and then smashed an officer to the ground with his rifle butt. The battle was over in an instant when the surviving Reb sharpshooters bolted out the back door and streaked for the brush.

"Hey, look," panted Sergeant Blett, pointing to some medical supplies in Union boxes that littered the floor. "This house was used by our boys as a hospital. They must have had to evacuate in a hurry to have left such valuable medicine behind."

"If ya ask me," spat Joe, "the sawbones' medicine ain't nothin' but poison! I best git me some o' them bandages, though."

The Bucktails had only occupied the house a short time when the building was rocked by a direct hit from a Confederate battery. After the dust and splinters had settled, the startled riflemen peered out a huge shell hole in the side wall. Then Jude shrieked, "Look! The Rebs jess brung their cannons forward. We'll be cut ta pieces if we stay here!"

"Jude's right!" growled Irvin. "Retreat!"

The First Rifles rushed back up the lane they had just cleared of enemy snipers, only pausing long enough to collect their wounded. Joe and Jude grabbed Zack by the armpits and skidded him behind them until they were out of range of the galling grapeshot spewed by the Rebel artillery. When they reached the safety of an oak grove, they sat Zack against the trunk of a sturdy tree. His pant leg was soaked with dark blood, so Joe cut it away with a pocketknife and cast the sodden cloth aside. What lay underneath caused the color to drain from Jack's face once he'd rushed to his brother's side. A Minie ball had shattered Zack's knee cap and implanted fragments of bone and shrapnel the length of his thigh. Blood gushed from the bullet hole until Joe cut a piece from his handkerchief and stuffed it in the wound. Next, he wound some clean bandage tightly around Zack's knee. The shrapnel wounds had already begun to crust over. Keener took out his pocket flash and poured whiskey on those until Zack screamed for him to stop.

The Bucktails dragged their casualties back to the turnpike where ambulances waited to cart them to the rear. Tearfully, Zack hugged his brothers before mumbling to Keener, "Thanks fer patchin' me up, Joe. I reckon you boys'll have ta fight the rest o' this here battle without me."

"The rest o' the war, ya mean," sobbed Jude.

"That's no way ta talk!" scolded Keener, pressing his flask into Zack's hands. "Drink this dry, laddie, an' ya won't mind so much what the sawbones does ta ya. Good luck. We'll come visit ya jess as soon as we kin."

"Yeah, good luck," cried Jack with tears streaming down his face.

"You'll have ta be the one leadin' the charges from now on, little brother," sighed Zack. "More luck ta you!"

Keener's squad moved sadly away and joined a crowd of Bucktails pressing back toward the battle front. They had just formed up with the rest of Meade's First Brigade when a brigade from Schenck's corps was pulled from the line and sent to plug a gap in Sigel's right flank. Before the Bucktails could fill the resulting void, a mob of screaming Rebs poured from the woods ahead and crashed into the hole. Keener, Sergeant Blett, and the others fired their Sharps until their gun barrels grew red hot, but still the Rebs came flooding through. The horde's gray coats took on a fur-like luster in the late morning sun. The Rebs' eyes shown like those of wolves smelling the blood of a deer they'd pulled down.

When General Meade saw his right flank crumbling, he ordered, amid a string of curses, "Fall back! Fall back!"

Coolly, the Bucktails retreated, firing as they went. They sent shot after deadly shot into the advancing Rebs. Soon, the gray ranks were forced to dodge for cover to escape the lethal storm of bullets raining down on them.

"That's fer you, Zack!" howled Jude, after his carefully squeezed shot sent a Reb sergeant sprawling on the ground.

"An' that, too!" screeched Jack, plugging a Confederate, who loped toward the shelter of a fallen log.

Meade cursed and cajoled until his command retreated safely across the turnpike to regroup with the rest of the Pennsylvania Reserves on a plateau near a bullet-riddled house. The First Brigade barely had time to catch its breath when word came again for them to attack. This time they were to support the Second and Third Brigades.

"Ain't it grand ta be at the rear o' the assault fer a change?" said Joe, boxing Jack on the shoulder in a friendly way.

"I jess wish Zack was here ta en-joy it," sobbed the lad. "I'm mighty fearful fer 'im."

"Zack's a tough nut!" replied Keener with an encouraging smile. "He'll be okay. Now, it's best ya keep yer head in this here battle, so you don't end up lyin' next ta 'im in the field hospital."

"You're right, Joe. Thanks."

The Bucktails, behind the Second and Third Brigades, dashed back down the hill, across the road, and on into the trees. They hadn't gone more than a couple hundred yards before the ranks ahead of them were raked by grapeshot and musket fire. Joe and Jack watched aghast as row after row of brave soldiers were mowed down in clouds of bloody spray. Before the Bucktails passed within cannon range and entered the terrible carnage, word for yet another retreat stopped the slaughter.

Keener returned from the woods in a daze. He couldn't remember the last time he'd eaten as he headed back up the plateau to reform with the others. His stomach churned from hunger and the turmoil of battle. Finally, he said to Jack, "Do you have a hard biscuit ya could spare, laddie?"

"Sorry, Joe. I give my last one ta Boone. He's the only one o' us I figgered had an appetite after all the killin' an' maimin' we seen taday. I still can't believe we lost both Zack an' Enos!"

"We done our share o' the fightin' fer sure. Keep yer chin up, Jack. We should be gettin' a break soon. It's almost dark."

"Then what's King's boys doin' over yonder ta our right?" asked Jude sourly.

"Why are you Bucktails dawdling there?" growled General Meade, riding angrily forward on his dusty mount. "Form up! There's work yet to be done! Forward!"

Once more the First Rifles tramped down the slope toward the distant Rebel lines. They met no resistance for the first mile, and the grim faces of Jack and Jude relaxed beneath their coats of gunpowder smoke. On the Bucktails strode with their Sharps cocked and ready. The twilight made the woods a murky place.

The riflemen continued on through the gloom, probing the shadows with their keen eyes. Suddenly, a volley rang out, and the astute skirmishers dove for cover. Soon, the very landscape was swarming with a gray tide that seemed to bubble up from the earth itself. Everywhere to the south there were flames spitting from the muskets of the advancing Rebels. There was so much lead in the air that the Bucktails dared not raise their Sharps to return fire. King's men took the brunt of the onslaught. The surprised infantry were blown down in gory heaps before they could break formation.

"Where did all them Rebs come from?" gasped Jack as a continuous barrage blew bark from the tree he cowered behind.

"Longstreet's here," said Sergeant Blett. "Now, our bacon's really fried."

"Retreat! Retreat!" floated the distant voice of General Meade as if from a dream.

"Good!" grunted Jude from behind an outcropping of rock. "The brass finally figgered we's been punished e-nough fer one day."

Each summer Union and Confederate reenactors recreate the famous battles of the Civil War on the actual fields where they occurred.

--Courtesy of Fay Leet

CHAPTER SEVENTEEN:
A NIGHTMARE OF A BATTLE

"We jess gits outta one trap, an' we's sent dead on inta another," groused Jude Swift.

"Amen to that," whispered Sergeant Blett, slinking ahead through the woods where his squad had been pinned down the evening before. "Maybe we'll be lucky this time. It looks like the Rebs slipped away after dark."

"Why can't King fetch out his own wounded?" complained Jack. "We always take care o' ours."

"That ain't the right attitude, laddie," scolded Keener. "Some o' them poor boys laid out here in the damp all night. If we don't help 'em, they's gonna die."

The Bucktails continued to sneak through the forest until dim moans directed their steps to the victims of the Reb attack. One-by-one they located the stricken soldiers and carried them to a sunlit glen. Boone was especially helpful in sniffing out the survivors amid the dead littering the gloomy groves. Keener also was relentless in his search, locating a wheezing, lung-shot corporal wedged beneath a fallen log. When twenty-five of King's casualties had been collected, the Bucktails combed the woods one last time to make sure no one had been missed. After Jude found two more dazed, shivering infantrymen concealed in a gully near a gurgling stream, McNeil sent a runner back to the Union lines to have the wounded transported to the field hospital.

Orders arrived soon after from General Meade directing the Bucktails to reconnoiter the ridge above Groveton. As the skirmishers moved out, Daniel Blett said, "You know, boys, this battle is like a recurring nightmare. Over and over we advance across the same ground only to end up where we began. This makes my dream of rats quite tame."

"We's fightin' rats, all right," grinned Joe, "but these rascals' bite is in their muskets."

The Bucktails moved warily forward through a battle-scarred wood and on up a sharp incline. They had barely reached the crest of the ridge when the firing of snipers concealed on their flanks sent them diving for cover. The familiar whine of bullets rent the air, followed by the deep boom of a distant Reb battery. The missiles flew thick and fast and from everywhere at once. With no visible target to shoot at, the Bucktails found themselves hopelessly pinned down.

Hugging the ground in frustration, Keener cried, "Unless Meade sends re-enforcements, we's gonna git our rears ventilated."

"Help is on the way!" shouted Daniel. "Look! Cooper's Battery is being brought up! And isn't that the Third Pennsylvania coming on the double-quick?"

"Charge!" howled Colonel McNeil. "Charge!"

Screeching like wildcats, the Bucktails leaped to their feet and swept across the ridge. With the Pennsylvania infantry in support, they dislodged the Reb sharpshooters from their hiding places and sent them hell-bent down the other side of the summit. Below them, the First Rifles could see the village of Groveton, and on the hill beyond, the previously hidden Reb battery.

After the Pennsylvania Reserves established their position on the ridgetop, the Bucktails were ordered to scout the distant town. Still flushed with victory, Keener and the others swooped down the densely wooded grade and into the village. Dodging from house to house, they soon discovered that the enemy had fled from there, too.

On the other side of Groveton, Colonel McNeil signaled for the men to halt. "We'd better proceed with caution," he directed. "A step at a time now, Bucktails."

Silently, the First Rifles spread into a thin skirmish line and crept across a brushy flat. Sticking to the cover, they slipped within fifty yards of a Reb field piece attended by a

134

lax cannon crew. As the Rebs jawed, joked, and chewed tobacco, the Bucktails encircled them in the stealthy manner of practiced deer hunters. When all were in place, McNeil motioned with his sword, and his skirmishers leaped from the thicket. Completely surrounded, the Confederate gunners could do nothing but gawk in surprise. When their sergeant finally did raise his pistol, Jack blew it out of his hand with a quick, instinctive shot. With the blood draining from their faces, the rest of the Rebs raised their hands and surrendered.

"Why don't we drag this here field piece with us?" jabbered Joe excitedly while rounding up the prisoners. "It'd make a dandy trophy fer us Bucktails."

"It's too heavy," overruled McNeil. "We'd better spike it instead."

"What's that mean?" asked Jack.

"We'll drive this down the touch hole," said Sergeant Blett, picking up a rusty, discarded bayonet. "That'll keep the Rebs from firing this cannon."

While Daniel hammered home the bayonet with his rifle butt, several men were singled out to accompany the prisoners back to the Union lines. Afterward, the remaining Bucktails were ordered forward by their colonel into an apple orchard. They had just entered the grove when a wave of gray infantry swept from the ridge beyond Groveton and assembled into battle formation. To the martial beat of drums, the Rebels advanced in an orderly fashion until within two hundred yards of the First Rifles.

Bunched together on open ground made the Confederates easy targets, and Keener and his mates whooped gleefully when they opened fire. The Bucktails continued to peddle lead until the shot-up Rebs broke rank and charged furiously. Running targets presented little challenge to the Pennsylvanians, either. Coolly they blazed away with their Sharps until mounting Reb casualties forced the enemy to retreat, dragging their dead behind them.

As another swarming mass of gray infantry began to assemble across the field, a courier galloped up to Colonel

McNeil and handed him a dispatch. After skimming the message, the Bucktail commander grunted, "We've been recalled, men. We'd better make a run for it before that horde charges us again."

A groan rose from the skirmishers before they took to their heels and sprinted from the apple grove. They burst through the quiet village and back up the ridge beyond. When they found the rise deserted, they fell panting to the ground. Finally, Jude gasped, "Where in tarnation did them Pennsylvania Reserves disappear to? I reckon they hung us out ta dry, as usual."

"There ain't nobody chasin' us," puffed Jack, glancing down the slope behind him. "Can't ya look at the bright side jess once, brother?"

"What bright side?" grumbled Jude. "Don't ya hear all that heavy firin' off ta the right there?"

"Well, that in itself is worth celebrating," smiled Sergeant Blett thinly. "At least we know where we need to get to."

Colonel McNeil allowed his spent men to catch their breath before ordering them back into rank. Carefully, they crept off the ridge in the direction of the distant battle. They had just rejoined the rest of the Pennsylvania Reserves on the top of Bald Hill when the firing to their right intensified to deafening proportions. Covering his ears to shut out the din, Sergeant Blett shouted, "It sounds like Porter's boys are getting all they can handle. Isn't that them coming on the run?"

"Even a brave hound kin only take so much maulin'," muttered Keener. "They's retreatin', all right."

The next instant, General Reynolds galloped from regiment to regiment imploring the Pennsylvania Reserves to rush to the aid of Porter's men below. The Bucktails, with the First Brigade, found the going rough. First, they had to struggle down a rugged ravine and across some very broken ground beyond. Next, they were met by a throng of panicked, retreating Federals, half of whom had discarded their weapons. After fighting through this mob, a Reb

136

battery raked the Bucktails with shot and shell, further impeding their progress. Stunned by the barrage, they milled about until Jude screeched, "Look, boys! The Third Brigade can't git off the hill. There's a passel o' Rebs hittin' 'em--hard!"

"Well, these Johnnies ain't 'zactly blowin' us kisses," growled Keener as another volley of grape tore through the ranks around him. "An' the Second Brigade's in the same pickle!"

Finding it futile to help Porter's Corps, General Reynolds herded his First and Second Brigades across a narrow dirt road and up the steep hillside beyond. There, he found a perfect defensive position among the rocks and trees.

"I think we've just retreated to Henry House Hill," panted Sergeant Blett, while he dug himself a rifle pit on the summit. "There was a lot of hard fighting here during the first Battle of Manassas. If we don't hold, boys, our army won't be able to retreat across Bull Run."

Keener and Jack hunkered behind a rock listening to the battle run its course on the hill across the road. The rumble of cannons soon gave way to the continuous roar of rifle volleys and then the occasional pop of scattered musket fire. When the shrill Rebel victory cry cut the air, Joe muttered, "Shoot straight when ya sees 'em comin', laddie. We's the last ones left ta stop 'em."

"I'll do what I kin," replied Jack. "Ya ain't seen me run yet, have ya?"

"Er me, neither," growled Jude from behind a neighboring granite outcrop.

"Give them hell!" roared Captain Irvin. "There's the damn Rebs now!"

To punctuate Irvin's command, Ransom's battery of field guns cut loose with a vicious roar at the first wave of enemy troops spilling from the opposite hilltop. Through shot and shell, they charged until the woods were alive with screeching Rebs. The gray ranks soon washed across the road below and advanced up the incline toward the dug-in Pennsylvania Reserves. The Confederate infantry scrambled over rocks and around trees, only pausing to fire and reload their muskets. Relentlessly, they climbed until the Union's first barrage ripped through their lines.

The Rebels fixed bayonets and charged on. Although Keener and his mates fired nonstop, they did little to discourage an enemy drunk on blood. Finally, Joe shouted, "Look at them rascals come at us! Fer every Reb I blow down, five more rush forward ta replace 'im."

"It's like trying to swat hornets swarming from a knocked down nest," whistled Sergeant Blett.

"An' the First and Second Pennsylvany is catchin' the worst o' it!" cried Jack. "They's startin' ta fall back!"

The other Bucktails glanced to their left in horror and saw the two regiments Jack pointed to buckle beneath the Rebel onslaught. When all seemed lost, General Reynolds snatched up the bullet-riddled colors of the Second Reserves and rode twice up and down the full length of his division line howling encouragement. Ignoring the Minie balls whizzing around him, the general waved the flag about his head until his cheering soldiers rallied and drove headlong into the superior Rebel ranks surging up the hill. Pushed back on their heels, the Confederate assault stalled and then fell grudgingly back.

In an instant, the Bucktails jumped up and sprinted down the hill. Going full-steam, they crashed into the Reb right flank, partially collapsing it. Bristling with fury, Jack and Jude knocked down men twice their size. Joe and Daniel, meanwhile, fought with veteran savvy, driving home their bayonets with efficient strokes. Growling like a rabid bulldog, Captain Irvin mowed down Rebs point-blank with his six shot Colt Army Revolver.

Suddenly, a Rebel even burlier than Keener leaped to cut Jack down with his saber. The blade hissed through the air, just missing the lad's neck by inches. Before the hulking lieutenant could slash at Swift again, Boone planted his teeth in the surprised man's forearm. Then, Jude drove his rifle butt into the officer's sternum, crashing him to the ground. Boone continued to spit and snarl over the gasping lieutenant until Jack shouted, "Come on, boy. He ain't gonna bother us no more. Here, boy."

Although badly outnumbered, the Pennsylvania Reserves fought with such tenacity that they drove the Rebels back down the slope and on across the road below. As darkness fell, the Rebs, badly mauled, retreated up the shadowy sides of Bald Hill. Near exhaustion, the Bucktails fired one last volley and then shook the dusk with a weary cheer.

"We held! We held!" cried Jack jubilantly as the last of the Rebs disappeared into the gloom.

"I'm proud o' ya, laddie!" exclaimed Keener, shaking Swift's hand. "Ya done real good. An' you, too, Jude!"

"Thanks, Joe," croaked the older boy. "I reckon that's the first compliment I ever got from a fella other than my brothers."

The Bucktails continued to stand guard along the road until the purposeful trod of marching feet approached from the north. Jack fidgeted in the dark as the column stomped closer and closer. Sweating despite the dampness of the night, he trained his Sharps up the road until he heard Sergeant Blett yelp, "It's Buchanan's brigade of regulars. We've been relieved, boys!"

Jack and the others formed up on the road and marched off to join the Union retreat. They plodded along in an orderly manner following the half asleep soldiers of Sykes' division. They splashed across a ford at Bull Run and proceeded in the dark to the east. Near Cub Run word finally passed down the ranks for the men to fall out. Wearily, they staggered into the shelter of a thick wood, wrapped themselves in their blankets, and fell instantly into unconsciousness.

Jack woke shivering the next morning, drenched by a cold rain that blew in at first light. He and his squad threw up a crude shelter made of canvas and a few tree limbs. Afterward, they gathered some dead twigs and in no time had a crackling fire going.

"It's too bad we don't have no coffee ta warm our

bones," said Keener, holding his huge paws over the flames.

"Don't worry, Joe. We're bound to get supplies now that the battle's over," replied Daniel.

"The gnawin' in my belly ain't goin' away 'til I finds out what happened ta Zack," muttered Jude.

"Then why don't we go look fer 'im?" suggested Keener. "Maybe we'll run inta the quartermaster on the way."

"We'd better ask Captain Irvin first," cautioned Blett.

"I can even tell you where to find Private Swift," said Irvin, from a group of officers gathered by a neighboring fire. "I was told that the field hospital is just up the pike toward Centreville. Give my regards to Zack if he hasn't already been moved to Washington."

Sergeant Blett's squad thanked Irvin, saluted, and headed off down the Warrenton Turnpike. They hadn't gone far before they saw a clump of dripping white tents off through the rain. Not bothering to avoid the puddles, they splashed from the road toward the surgeons' tent.

"Do you have a Private Zack Swift here?" asked Daniel when they had gained admittance.

"Let me check the roll," replied a doctor wearing thick spectacles. "Yes, here's his name. I'll send an attendant with you."

"Thank ya, sir," replied Jack. "He-e's my brother, an' we's all worried sick 'bout 'im."

The attendant led the Bucktails down a long line of tents filled with suffering men. As they tiptoed along, they could hear the patients uttering prayers, hurling curses, or crying feverishly for loved ones. When they reached the last enclosure, the attendant pointed inside with a sad look etched on his face. Immediately, Jack and Jude ducked inside and began scanning the cots for Zack.

"O-O-Over here," called a weak voice. "Why, it's my brothers. Brothers!"

The Swifts rushed to the side of a fellow shrouded to the chin in a raveled wool blanket. His oval face was pale as death, and the eyes protruded abnormally above a drooling, wide-set mouth.

"I-I-Is that really you, Zack!" gasped Jack, unable to mask his horror.

"Yeah, little brother. I done sur-vived the sawbones."

"How's ya doin?" asked Joe, sidling around the Swifts to the foot of the cot.

"I reckon I won't be playin' no more baseball," whimpered Zack, pulling back the blanket to reveal a bandaged stump where his leg used to be. "Er doin' nothing useful fer that matter. I-I-I don't know what's ta become o' me."

"Can't you go home to your father?" asked Sergeant Blett, swallowing hard. "Surely, he'll put you up until you recover."

Pointing to the scar on his cheek, Zack mumbled, "He figgered I was useless when I was whole. He done that ta me jess fer playin' horseshoes with the set he made fer Widow Rice's nag. What's he gonna think o' me now?"

"No, he can't go home," seconded Jude with a brooding frown. "Not as unfergivin' as Pap is."

"Then he can go stay with my folks!" exclaimed Keener. "My father has been lookin' fer someone to help him run his mill. I ain't cut out fer that there work, but a bright fella like Zack would be."

"Ya think so?" asked Swift after a smile flickered across his wan lips.

"Sure. There ain't no heavy work in-volved. Ya jess gotta learn how the machinery works an' order other fellas ta do yer biddin'. I'm sure Father would be glad ta help a war hero like yerself. I'll set down taday an' write 'im a letter ta introduce ya."

"You'd do that fer me?"

"Sure as shootin' I would!"

"An' I'll send ya some o' my pay ta tide ya over," promised Jack.

"Me, too," said Jude. "I ain't got no drinkin' habit like Keener there, er a gal ta eat it up, neither."

"T-T-Thanks, boys," sputtered Zack, bursting into tears. "But don't ya go sayin' nothin' 'bout Joe's boozin'. If he hadn't give me that flask o' his, I reckon I'd never got through all that hackin' they done. . . on my leg. . . "

After an awkward silence Sergeant Blett said, "I have friends in the U.S. Sanitary Commission in Washington. I'll write them. They'll make sure you get the best care available in the city."

"Really?"

"Of course," replied Daniel. "Nothing's too good for a fellow Bucktail."

"That's right!" enthused Keener. "All o' us fightin' wildcats is brothers."

"Oh, and Captain Irvin sends his regards," added Blett with an encouraging smile. "He's a fine gentleman. I know he'll help you any way he can, Zack."

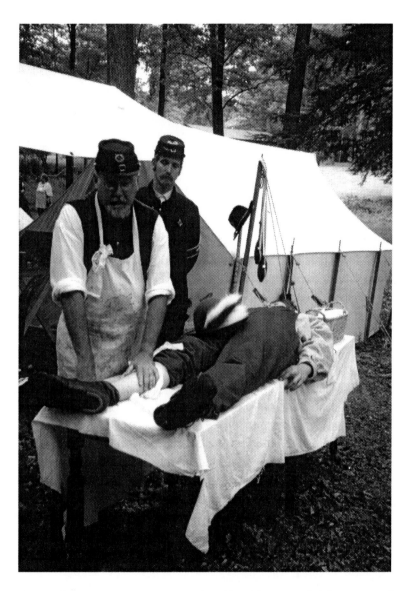

(l-r) Surgeon reenactor, John Warsing, and his steward assistant, Joel Coudriet, attend to Waylon Walck during a demonstration at the 2004 Bucktail Reunion held in Curwensville, PA.   In the Civil War leg wounds usually required amputation because Minie balls would shatter the bones they struck.

CHAPTER EIGHTEEN:
A COMIC REUNION

Still visibly shaken by their hospital visit with Zack, the Swift brothers plodded dejectedly down the road to the east later that morning with the rest of the Bucktails. A pall of gloom clouded their faces, and their long mouths arched into bitter frowns. Finally, Jude yelled in a fit of rage, "It jess ain't fair what happened ta Zack! How kin God take away from a fella the best gift He give 'im?"

"Yeah!" cried Jack. "My big brother was always the fastest an' best at any game we played. He never showed no pride in it neither er bullied anyone 'cause o' it."

"Maybe God has another plan for Zack," said Sergeant Blett softly. "If he does well at the Keeners' mill, he'll make way more money than he could with his athletic skills. I'd encourage all you boys to learn a trade. Then, you'll never have to worry about getting by."

"Maybe we could come work fer you after the war," suggested Jack. "Makin' carriages would be a dandy job!"

"Yeah, I've always liked woodcarvin' an' such," mumbled Jude. "I might be interested, too."

"As restless as you is, I reckon that job wouldn't be good fer you boys," smirked Joe. "Why, you'd be takin' off in the first coach ya done built, an' Daniel wouldn't see hide ner hair o' ya ag'in."

"Don't listen to him," chuckled Blett. "You know, I should be able to take on an apprentice or two when all those generals return home with their discharge pay. I'll definitely keep you in mind."

The cold drizzle that accompanied the Bucktails on their march soon put an end to conversation. On the column

144

trudged through red mud up to their ankles until they saw the smoking chimneys of a little village ahead. A sign announced the place as Centreville, and the First Rifles thankfully fell out of line at the command of Colonel McNeil. Several covered wagons were drawn up in the town square distributing food to another Union regiment. When the Bucktails' turn came, they crowded hungrily around the quartermaster's unit and drew their first hardtack and salt beef since going into combat four days before.

"Hey, where's our coffee ration?" snarled Keener angrily.

"You'll be getting it, Private," snapped a surly supply sergeant. "Keep your pants on."

"That'd be a lot easier ta do if we was fed reg'lar," replied Keener. "I've took my belt in so many times, it coils 'round me like a dang constrictor snake."

"Ya know how them quartermasters done got their names, don't ya?" muttered Jude.

"No," said Daniel innocently. "Why don't you tell us."

"It's 'cause they only gives us boys a quarter o' the supplies an' keeps the rest fer theirselves."

The Bucktails moved away laughing at Jude's remark. Hungrily, they chomped on their hard biscuits and washed them down with stale water from their canteens. They were too starved to complain about the weevils in their food. They continued to wolf down their rations until they were herded into marching formation and hustled back down the road toward the battleground they had just left.

"Here we go marchin' in circles ag'in," groaned Jude. "Don't tell me the Rebs still ain't got a belly full after three days o' hard fightin'."

"They's always thirsty fer Yankee blood," assured Keener. "I jess hope they don't drink none o' mine."

"They'd git a cheap drunk if they did," said Jude wryly.

"Hey, lay off Joe," chided Jack. "Sometimes I think you're like a rattler with a broken back, strikin' at anything 'round it. I sure hope ya find somethin' ta make ya happy, brother, be-fore we shoots ya ourselves ta save the Rebs the trouble."

The Bucktails and the Pennsylvania Reserves were pushed up the road to Cub Run on the double-quick. When they arrived at the creek bank, they could see a company of Rebels advancing in the forest on the opposite side of the steam. Cussing furiously, General Meade deployed his troops into battle formation and then ordered Ransom's battery to cut loose at the enemy. The field guns sent barrage after barrage screaming into the far woods to blow down trees and rip up the earth. The cannons belched and thundered for over an hour uncontested by the Confederates. Finally, Meade howled for the artillery to cease firing. All became silent and remained so until darkness spread from the mountains to the west.

"What do ya think be-come o' them Rebs?" asked Jack, peering bug-eyed off through the gloom.

"That musta been Jackson's rear guard," replied Joe. "By now, they's probably halfway back ta Richmond. I'll bet they's still laughin' over all that ammunition our artillery done wasted killin' trees."

The Bucktails remained on alert all night. A dense fog replaced the afternoon rain and made the pickets even jumpier than usual. Several times shots rang out when sentries mistook the scurry of nocturnal beasts for a Reb attack.

"It's darker than the inside of a cow," whispered Sergeant Blett, after one such disturbance.

"An' it's udderly annoyin'," chortled Keener.

The first light of morning confirmed that the Rebels had evacuated the area. Meade sent a party of scouts to make doubly sure. Afterward, he ordered his men to pull out. The Pennsylvania Reserves stomped woodenly back to Centreville. Instead of receiving a deserved rest, they tramped on the rest of the day to Fairfax Court House. There, the men fairly collapsed from the ranks when dismissed. Not bothering to erect tents or even eat dinner, Keener's squad fell instantly asleep in a field on the outskirts of town.

Daybreak found the men still barely able to function. The officers barked and threatened before the Bucktails groggily swayed to their feet and got in line. The march resumed soon after. On and on the men trudged until they arrived at Alexandria where the rest of the Union Army was bivouacked. On the perimeter of the Federal's tent city, Colonel McNeil ordered the men to set up camp.

Wearily, Keener and his squad erected their dog houses and gathered firewood from a neighboring cherry grove. They had just started their dinner fires when they saw Lieutenant Colonel Kane's battalion tramping up the regimental street. In an instant, Joe and the others leaped up to cheer and to scan the depleted ranks for long-separated friends.

Kane ordered Companies C, G, H, and I into parade formation. They snapped to attention as McNeil emerged from his headquarters. After a brief inspection, the colonel dismissed the men by shouting, "Welcome back, Bucktails. Those Rebs better be wary now that we're together again. Victorious days are ahead, I can assure you. Fall out now and get reacquainted with your brothers-in-arms."

The next hour was spent shaking hands and swapping news and battle yarns as the long separated companies intermingled. Often, Keener saw his pal, Hosea Curtis, in the milling mob. Each time he rushed to greet him, another group of back-slapping friends would cut him off. Finally, as dusk fell, Kane's men were ordered away to set up their own camp. Groaning with disappointment, Joe muttered to Daniel Blett, "I reckon I'll have ta intraduce ya to Curtis another time. He could teach ya a thing er two 'bout bein' a sergeant. An' bein' a private, too, after all the times he lost his stripes fer bustin' army rules."

"Sounds like an interesting fellow," replied Blett. "He must be a born leader if the brass keep promoting him again."

When Joe and Daniel meandered back to their bivouac, they found the Swift brothers gorging on bacon, potatoes, and fresh beef. After shaking his head in disbelief, Keener said, "Am I hallucinatin' er what? Where did you boys git them vittles?"

"A supply wagon come by while you was gone," replied Jack between bites. "We drew rations fer you boys, too, no questions asked."

"With Washington just across the river," grinned Daniel, "we should get all the food we can bolt down. I sure hope we stay here a long time. I owe my dear wife, Catherine, many letters and myself a hundred missed meals."

After the Bucktails had stuffed themselves, they crawled into their dog tents and fell into a deep, contented sleep. Warmed by a balmy breeze, their snores went unbroken until the sun was high in the sky the next morning. Even the officers slept in and didn't hold roll call until everyone had enjoyed a hearty breakfast. Then the men were taken to headquarters to draw their long-delayed pay. Afterward, they were given the rest of the day off.

"Dang!" shouted Joe, fanning himself with a handful of greenbacks. "Is I gonna have a hot time taday!"

"Kin I come, too?" asked Jack. "I wanna go meet Boone an' see ya put 'im in his place."

"Uh, I got some things ta attend to first," grinned Keener. "Maybe this evenin' we'll pay old Crossmire a visit."

"Come on, Jack. Let's go look at the riverboats," said Jude. "You don't wanna hang 'round that fella with all that money burnin' a hole in his pocket. Who knows what bad habits he might intraduce ya to."

"See you boys later," cackled Joe. "Much later!"

Whistling a happy drinking song, Keener ambled to the end of the regimental street where a group of sutlers had set up shop. Casually, he approached a familiar gent and said, "Do you have any pocket flasks? I give mine ta a sick friend."

"Plenty of them, Captain," replied the sutler. Curling the end of his handlebar moustache with nicotine-stained fingers, he added, "Even if you lost your old one to the Washington police."

"An' how 'bout somethin' ta put in it?"

"Oil of gladness doesn't come cheap, Captain."

"After the campaign I done fought, I'd even settle fer forty-rod," chortled Keener, slipping the fellow three crisp greenbacks.

"I'll see what I can do. Yes, indeed!"

With an even wider grin, Keener returned to the Bucktail camp. He took a long pull from his new flask and then concealed it in his coat. He proceeded down the street until he heard some boisterous voices coming from inside a wedge tent. Joe ducked inside the smoky interior and found a group of corporals engaged in a game of poker. The soldiers took one look at the wad of bills Keener produced from his pocket and invited him to play, despite his private's rank.

Joe won three hands in a row with superior cards and two more by bluffing. When he had doubled his cash, he stashed the bills in his pocket and rose to leave. "Thanks fer the game, fellas," he chuckled. "See ya ag'in sometime."

"Hey, you can't leave with all our greenbacks, Private!" shouted a squat, muscular corporal, his face turning crimson.

"It's a free country," replied Keener evenly, bunching up his ham-sized fist. "At least here in the North it is."

"But I want a chance ta win back my money!"

"How good is ya at fightin'? That's what it'll take!"

When Joe stood up, his hulking frame filled up the entire entranceway. He glared menacingly at the corporal until the latter gulped twice and stammered, "I-I-I guess I'll have ta ketch ya on a day ya ain't so lucky. That time's comin', sure as s-s-shootin'."

"I reckon that'll be when I's too drunk ta read the cards," grinned Keener. "See ya then, Corporal."

Joe returned to the regimental street and made his way toward a group of soldiers crowded around a rubber blanket laid on the ground. The blanket had different numbers on it. The men placed their money on these numbers while another fellow threw dice. He hadn't gone more than a couple of steps toward these Chuck-or-Luck players before he saw a familiar group of Bucktails stomping dejectedly from the game. A monstrous sergeant was leading the way. Behind him came a lean, hawk-nosed corporal and three privates. The first of the privates wore spectacles. The other two were tall and wiry but of totally different demeanors. While one wore a sober expression, the other continually flashed a gap-toothed grin.

Keener strode up to the giant sergeant and clamped him roughly in a bear hug that would have broken most men's ribs. "How ya doin' there, Hosea?" he bawled. "I ain't seen ya in a coon's age."

"Boys," wheezed Curtis when he'd been released from the other's powerful grasp, "I'd like ya ta meet Joe Keener."

Bucky Culp and Jimmy Jewett's eyes got big as cannon balls, while the serious Frank Crandall backed away from Keener like he was a gorilla that had escaped from a zoo. Only the smirking Boone Crossmire stood his ground and said, "Glad ta finally meet ya, Joe. You're a big un. I didn't think manure could be piled that high."

Keener's eyes narrowed dangerously, and a growl rumbled in his throat. All at once he gave Boone a playful slap that knocked him halfway across the road. Afterward, he thundered good-naturedly, "You gotta be Boone 'cause Hosea said you was crazy. Ain't no other monkey-faced private in this army--or any other--would dare sass me like that if he wasn't."

"I think when the war ends, I'm gonna get ya real mad at me, Keener," replied Boone as he rose to his feet and dusted himself off.

"Why's that, little man?"

"'Cause you'd knock me all the way back ta McKean County, an' think o' all the shoe leather I'd save."

"Yeah, but you'd land so hard, it'd take ya twice as long ta climb outta the hole ya made as it would ta walk there."

"I jess wonder how a big fella like you hides on the battlefield. You're wider than any oak tree an' too tall ta hunker behind a fence. That must mean you're dang good at dodgin' bullets."

"I don't have ta dodge 'em, Boone. When this here war started, I ate bullets fer breakfast 'til I de-veloped an immunity to 'em. You know. Like some fellas do ta rattlesnake poison."

"Well, Joe, ya got me there," laughed Boone. "But that don't mean I'm surrenderin'. We got a long war ahead o' us, an' I'm as full o' banter as most generals are o' hot air."

"Yeah, but at least we kin call a truce long enough fer me ta shake yer hand."

"Sorry, Joe, but I'd rather have Hosea slam my hand in a tavern door than risk that grip o' yers. Why don't we jess exchange salutes an' be done with it?"

Boone's suggestion precipitated a series of slapstick salutes that had the rest of the squad doubled over with laughter. First, Boone gave a lopsided salute over the bridge of his nose. Joe answered with an off-center salute to the eye. Then Boone saluted from his Adam's apple and pretended to choke, which caused Joe to salute so hard he knocked off his hat, sending his shock of red hair tumbling down over his eyes.

When Boone bent over and saluted from his rear, Sergeant Curtis croaked, "That's enough, you two. If we don't separate ya soon, we's gonna be too laughed out ta shoot them new Sharps. Come along, Boone. Let's go have us some grub. See ya in the wash, Joe."

"Okay, Hosea. Don't fergit ta bring yer own soap."

Dang, thought Keener, as his Company I friends strag-gled away, I didn't git ta bust on Crossmire fer us namin' our mascot after 'im. Oh well, there'll be plenty o' time fer that now us Bucktails is back tagether ag'in.

CHAPTER NINETEEN:
KEENER'S SADNESS

"What's all this here sudden interest in drillin'?" asked Joe after marching and maneuvering on the Alexandria parade grounds the whole next morning.

"It's because General McClellan's been placed back in charge of our army," replied Sergeant Blett. "You know how much Little Mac stresses discipline."

"An' bustin' our backs in the process," grumbled Jude.

"It looks like I won't be leading you on any more drills," sighed Blett. "I've just been transferred to Company F because the Carbon County boys need an experienced soldier to whip them into shape. The brass promoted me to First Sergeant."

"Well, congratulations!" cried Jack.

"Yeah, an' good luck," grinned Keener, shaking Daniel's hand.

"I think your luck's about to improve, too, Joe," winked Blett.

"The only way that'd happen is if it rained corn squeezin's from the sky!"

When Keener and the rest of Company K returned to their bivouac, they found a squad of recruits waiting for them. The newcomers were a nondescript lot except for a gaunt, dark-haired private with a pug nose and a fastidiously clean-shaven face. The man preened and puffed on a cigar as though he were higher bred than the rest of his fellows. Boone's fur raised on his back, and he emitted a low growl when the private produced a sharp toad-stabber and began picking the dirt from beneath his fingernails with it.

Captain Irvin was with the recruits, and he said to Joe,

"Sergeant Keener, I'd like you to meet your new squad."

"What do ya mean by that, sir?"

"I mean with Sergeant Blett leaving, we need a battle-tested veteran to whip these boys into fighting shape. You're Company K's most experienced enlisted man, so you've been promoted."

"But, sir," protested Joe, "what do I know 'bout leadin' other fellas?"

"By the way you brought Private Swift out of the hellfire of the Peninsula, I'd say plenty! Here are your stripes. Have them sewn on by our next drilling session. Dismissed!"

Dejectedly, Keener took the stripes from his captain and then ran his eyes over the nine new soldiers he had been assigned. Eight of them were sober men of various statures that Joe figured were straight from lumber camps or dirt farms. Their muscles were well defined and their eyes dull as oxen. It was the lean ninth man, however, who looked to be the real scrapper of the lot. His pug nose and sardonic leer reminded Keener of the prize fighters he'd seen displayed on handbills.

"Say, Sergeant," said the gaunt private, "my name is Samuel Whalen. I'd be glad ta sew them stripes on yer jacket fer ya. I'm mighty good with needles an' such."

Boone's hackles rose at the first sound of the man's oily voice. Jack had to restrain the hound before he stopped growling.

"Okay, Whalen," replied Keener, ignoring the mascot's snarls. "My fingers is big around as sausages. I can't even grip no needle, let alone work it."

"Hey, why didn't ya ask me?" protested Jack. "I'da done that sewin' fer ya, Joe."

"No, I already give the job ta Whalen. But I'm glad you an' Jude's still in my squad. It'll be nice ta have a coupla broke-in fellas ta help me."

"It'll take more 'n' that," assured Jude, "if ya trust that slick fella with anything more 'n' latrine duty."

Whalen shot the Swift brothers a menacing glare before

sitting against a tree trunk to sew. Joe formed up the other members of the squad to practice the manual of arms.

"We know this here drill in our sleep," protested Jude. "Why do we gotta do it when that Whalen fella gits ta sit out?"

"'Cause I'm sergeant is why. Present arms!"

Samuel took his sweet time attaching Keener's stripes, only finishing as the drilling concluded. Then he took two cigars from his pocket, offering the fatter one to Joe. "Here's yer coat, Sergeant," he gobbled. "An' take this cigar with my compliments ta yer drillin' skill. I know I come ta the right squad with an accomplished fella like you leadin' it."

"Why, thank ya, Private Whalen. Did ya git yer rations okay when ya come inta camp?"

"Yes, sir. I'm all set up. Yes, indeedy."

Jack and Jude scowled at the new private, noting the glint of silver in his crocodile smile. When dismissed from rank, they brushed furiously past him with the bristling Boone at their heels.

The next morning was hot and sticky when orders came for the Union Army to break camp. Soon, the entire landscape was full of tramping blue troops. After crossing the Potomac River, the army was broken into columns and sent down five parallel roads toward Frederick, Maryland. The Bucktails ate the dust of a multitude of marching men. Even the veterans wilted in the mugginess of the afternoon.

Jack Swift was having a particularly difficult time keeping up. His breath came in short spasms, and his complexion was the color of dough. He stumbled blindly along with his head swimming and clammy sweat seeping from his hat band. When he reached to take a pull from his canteen, his feet got tangled with those of Whalen, who had been inching closer to him. In the next instant, Jack pitched headlong on the road and lay in a crumbled heap.

"Hey, Whalen, ya done that ta my brother on purpose," accused Jude.

"Done what?" asked Samuel innocently.

"Tripped 'im is what!"

"Hey, what's the de-lay?" growled Keener, plodding back to see why his squad had stopped to snarl up the entire column.

"Whalen tripped my brother. I think Jack's hurt bad!" shouted Jude.

"Did not, Sergeant!" cried Samuel. "The heat musta got 'im."

"An' yer foot!"

"Knock it off!" ordered Joe. "We can't hold up the whole dang army. You boys'll have ta carry Private Swift. Git 'im up!"

"But why can't we rest in the shade fer a while?" asked Jude.

"Ain't ya heared? Bobbie Lee done in-vaded the North, an' we's been sent ta stop 'im. Git yer brother up. Now!"

"But I jess 'bout had it, too," whined Whalen. "Couldn't ya git one o' them bigger fellas ta help 'im, Sergeant? Please."

"Okay, Baker, give Swift a hand. Let's go."

Jude, Baker, and the other strapping recruits took turns half-dragging and half-carrying Jack for the rest of the afternoon. By the time the sun mercifully dropped below the horizon, all were completely spent except for Whalen. After being dismissed from the ranks, Jack's nurses listlessly prepared a smelly stew with ingredients they contributed from their haversacks. Jude also tended to his younger brother until the lad finally sat up and took a sip of water.

The whole time Samuel sat smoking with his back against a tree. When dinner was ready, he sauntered over and began helping himself to a hearty portion until Jude snapped, "What do ya think you're doin'?"

"What's it look like? I'm gettin' me some o' this hellfire stew."

"Did ya help pre-pare it?"

"No, but I'm part o' this here squad, ain't I?"

"Yeah! When it's convenient fer ya!" thundered Jude, knocking Whalen's plate out of his hand.

Swift doubled up his fists and lunged toward Samuel. Before he could deliver a blow, his antagonist pulled a knife and thrust it within an inch of Jude's stomach. With a surprised cry, Jude jerked back, looking for a weapon to defend himself. Whalen lashed out a second time, renting the boy's baggy coat sleeve. A third thrust missed Jude's cheek by a quarter of an inch.

"Ya like pickin' on fellas, don't ya?" croaked Jude to buy himself some time.

"You betcha!" crowed Whalen. "'Specially boys pretendin' ta be men."

"Ya probably like slappin' 'round yer own son, too, if ya got one."

"I'd have ta have a mighty long arm ta do that," sneered Samuel, "with him livin' in Smethport. I reckon I'll jess have ta settle fer hurtin' you."

"Hey, my own pap did e-nough o' that!" snarled Jude, edging toward the campfire. "I'll never let ya touch me, ya weasel!"

Angrily, Swift reached down into the fire and snatched up a long tree branch that burned brightly on one end. He waved it wildly at Samuel, somehow managing to knock off his assailant's hat.

With the scent of singed hair strong in his nostrils, Whalen dodged deftly to the side and then lunged to disable the boy. Suddenly, Boone came leaping over the fire pit and planted his fangs in the man's leg. Whalen coolly diverted the thrust meant for Jude into the mascot's rib cage. The hound yelped once and crashed thrashing to the ground.

"Now, what's goin' on?" shouted Sergeant Keener, bursting from the darkness. "Can't Captain Irvin call me away fer one second without some ruckus breakin' out?"

Bug-eyed, the squad watched Boone struggle in his death throes. Finally, Whalen said, "Swift an' that dang hound attacked me, Sergeant. I was forced ta de-fend myself."

"Is that what happened, Jude?" asked Keener. "What do you have ta say?"

"W-W-Whalen's been askin' fer it all day! He can't git away with hurtin' my little brother. An' gittin' out o' every duty. I-I-I jess can't put up with it!"

"An' he should be whipped fer killin' our dog," gasped Jack weakly from his blanket.

"How 'bout the rest o' you men?" asked the sergeant. "What kin you tell me 'bout what happened here?"

Wiping the blood from his knife, Samuel glared menacingly at his fellow recruits. After none of them dared answer, Joe said, "Whalen, put that toad-stabber away. Bein' I wasn't here ta see what caused this here trouble, I reckon my hands is tied. Okay, men, all o' ya best turn in. We's got us another long march tomorrow, an' I don't want no one fallin' out o' rank like taday. We'll bury Boone in the mornin' be-fore we leave. If there's any more fightin', I swear I'll punish the whole lot o' ya!"

In stunned silence, the squad rolled into their blankets and huddled around the fire to think about what they'd just heard and seen. As the men turned in, Keener stooped over Jack and mumbled apologetically, "Sorry 'bout Boone, laddie. I'm also sorry I couldn't help ya more when ya co-llapsed taday. Now, that I'm sergeant, I gotta look out fer all the men, not jess you."

"I kin see that things is gonna change," sniffed Jack. "Maybe it's best if me an' my brother transfer inta Sergeant Blett's outfit."

"But why would ya wanna leave after all we been through tagether?"

"'Cause I smell trouble that don't seem ta git up yer nostrils. I'm gonna see Captain Irvin tomorrow 'bout transferrin'. I'll tell 'im how Daniel promised us a job after the war. After I ex-plain that it only makes sense fer me an' Jude ta stick by the sergeant, I reckon Irvin can't refuse our re-quest. I'll never fergit ya, Joe, sure as shootin'."

"Goodbye, then, Jack," said Keener sadly, patting the lad on the shoulder. "I reckon I can't make ya stay on if Daniel Blett will take ya inta his company."

"Hey, don't worry 'bout them leavin', Sergeant,"

whispered the oily voice of Samuel Whalen from the neighboring shadows. "I'll stick by ya, sir. You kin count on me bein' a real pal."

Joe closed his eyes and listened to the flames lick from the nearby fire pit. A forlorn feeling gripped him as he rose to go make his own bed. Grim memories haunted him from the bloody Peninsula Campaign and even grimmer prospects loomed ahead in the mountains and rolling farmland of Maryland. He walked stiffly away, unaware of the tears that flowed down his ruddy, massive cheeks.

Edward A. Irvin was just 23 years old when he signed the muster roll of the Company K Bucktails and was elected their captain. After the Second Battle of Bull Run, his fortunes of war took a deadly turn when he was severely wounded at the Battle of South Mountain and again at the Battle of Fredericksburg. Due to these wounds, he was eventually discharged from service on May 1, 1863. Afterward, Irvin worked in the lumber business and later was elected to the Pennsylvania Senate. He died on October 13, 1908. His grave is located at Oak Hill Cemetery in Curwensville, PA.

BIBLIOGRAPHY

Angle, Paul M. <u>A Pictorial History of the Civil War Years</u>. Garden City,
  NY: Doubleday & Company, Inc., 1967.

Athearn, Robert G. <u>The Civil War</u>. New York: Choice Publishing, Inc.,
  1988.

Aubrecht, Michael, "Civil War Baseball: Baseball and the Blue and Gray,"
  <www.baseballalmanac.com/articles/aubrecht2004b.shtml>
  (14 March 2005).

"Baseball," <u>Compton's Encyclopedia</u>, Vol. 3 (1984), pp. 87-96.

Bates, Samuel P. <u>History of Pennsylvania Volunteers 1861-1865</u>.
  5 vols. Harrisburg: B. Singerly, State Printer, 1869.

---. <u>Martial Deeds of Pennsylvania</u>. Philadelphia: T. H. Davis Company,
  1876.

Botkin, B. A., ed. <u>A Civil War Treasury of Tales, Legends and Folklore</u>.
  New York: Random House, 1960.

Bowman, John S., ed. <u>The Civil War Day By Day</u>. Greenwich, CT:
  Dorset Press, 1989.

Brandt, Dennis W. "The Bucktail Regiment." <u>Potter County Historical
  Society QuarterlyBulletin</u>, January 1998, pp. 2-3.

Catton, Bruce. <u>The Army of the Potomac: Mr. Lincoln's Army</u>. Garden
  City, NY: Doubleday & Company, Inc., 1962.

Chamberlin, Lieutenant-Colonel Thomas. <u>History of the One Hundred
  and Fiftieth Regiment Pennsylvania Volunteers, Second Regiment, Bucktail Brigade</u>. Philadelphia: F. McManus, Jr. & Company, 1905.

Commager, Henry Steele. <u>The Blue and the Gray</u>. 2 vols. New York:
  The Fairfax Press, 1982.

Davis, William C. The Battlefields of the Civil War. London: Salamander Books Limited, 1999.

---. The Commanders of the Civil War. London: Salamander Books Limited, 1999.

---. The Fighting Men of the Civil War. London: Salamander Books Limited, 1999.

Garrison, Webb. Civil War Curiosities. Nashville: Rutledge Hill Press, 1994.

---. More Civil War Curiosities. Nashville: Rutledge Hill Press, 1995.

Guernsey, Alfred H. and Henry M. Alden. Harper's Pictorial History of The Civil War. New York: The Fairfax Press, 1866.

*Glover, Edwin A. Bucktailed Wildcats: A Regiment of Civil War Volunteers. New York: Thomas Yoseloff, 1960.

History of the Counties of McKean, Elk, Cameron and Potter, Pennsylvania. 2 vols. Chicago: J.H. Beers & Co. Publishers, 1890.

Kelly, Brian C. Best Little Stories from the Civil War. Nashville: Cumberland House, 1998.

"Letters of the Civil War." Hartford Courant, 24 July 1862, pg. 2, col. 2.

Lord, Francis A. Civil War Collector's Encyclopedia. New York: Castle Books, 1965.

McPherson, James M., ed. The American Heritage New History of the Civil War. New York: Penguin Books, 1996.

*Means, William W. Corporal Brewer, A Bucktail Survivor. 2 vols. Lincoln: Writers Club Press, 2000.

Nofi, Albert A. The Civil War Treasury. New York: Mallard Press, 1990.

O'Shea, Richard. Battle Maps of the Civil War. Tulsa: Council Oak Books, 1992.

Robertson, William P. and David Rimer. <u>The Bucktails' Shenandoah March</u>. Shippensburg, PA: White Mane Publishing Company, 2002.

Schroeder, Patrick A. <u>Pennsylvania Bucktails: A Photographic Album of the 42nd, 149th & 150th Regiments</u>. Daleville, VA: Schroeder Publications, 2001.

Stern, Phillip Van Doren, ed. <u>Soldier Life in the Union and Confederate Armies</u>. Bloomington: Indiana University Press, 1961.

Stone, Rufus Barrett. <u>McKean: The Governor's County</u>. New York: Lewis Historical Publishing Company, Inc., 1926.

Tanner, Robert G. <u>Stonewall in the Valley</u>. Garden City, New York: Doubleday & Company, Inc., 1976.

<u>The Union Army</u>. 8 vols. Madison, WI: Federal Publishing Company, 1908.

*Thomson, O. R. Howard and William H. Rauch. <u>History of the Bucktails</u>. Philadelphia: Electric Printing Company, 1906.

Ward. Geoffrey C. <u>The Civil War: An Illustrated History</u>. New York: Alfred A. Knopf, Inc., 1990.

Warner, Ezra J. <u>Generals in Blue</u>. Baton Rouge: Louisiana State University Press, 1964.

*These sources provided the portions of dialogue attributed to real-life officers that appear in this novel.

AUTHOR PROFILE:
DAVID RIMER

Currently retired, David Rimer taught speech and English for thirty-four years at Bradford Area High School in Bradford, PA. He received his BS degree from Clarion University, an MEd from Edinboro University, and further graduate credits at St. Bonaventure, Gannon University, and East Stroudsburg University. David and his wife Marcia live in Bradford, PA. They have one daughter, Stephanie. Mr. Rimer has edited several books for Robyl Press and is a published mystery author. He began collaborating with William P. Robertson in 1989 and cowrote six other Bucktail novels:

Hayfoot, Strawfoot: The Bucktail Recruits (White Mane Publishing, 2002)
The Bucktails' Shenandoah March (White Mane Publishing, 2002)
The Bucktails' Antietam Trials (White Mane Publishing, 2006)
The Battling Bucktails at Fredericksburg (White Mane Publishing, 2006)
The Bucktails at the Devil's Den
The Bucktails' Last Call

AUTHOR PROFILE:
WILLIAM P. ROBERTSON

William P. Robertson graduated from Mansfield University in 1972 with a BS in English. Since then he has worked in factories, taught high school English, and run a successful house painting business. He began freelancing short stories, poetry, and articles in 1978 and has been published in over 480 magazines in the U.S., Canada, England, Scotland, Ireland, Wales, Romania, Australia, New Zealand, and Malaysia. He has also published eleven collections of poetry, two audio books of horror verse, two volumes of short stories, and two Civil War novels. In his spare time Bill enjoys photography, trout fishing, and Civil War reenacting. He belongs to the Company I Bucktail unit of McKean County in Pennsylvania.

ALSO FROM INFINITY PUBLISHING

<u>Lurking in Pennsylvania</u> collects three decades of William P. Robertson's best horror stories and poems, many of which appeared in magazines worldwide. In this anthology Bill writes understated Gothic terror in the tradition of Lovecraft and Poe. He draws his material from local legends, his grandma's Swedish folktales, and traumatic personal experiences. He also delves into dark humor and lends a fresh perspective to the werewolf and troll. Bill's best work chills rather than sickens. To order an autographed copy of <u>Lurking in Pennsylvania</u>, send $15.27 (postpaid) to William P. Robertson, P.O. Box 293, Duke Center, PA 16729. Make checks payable to the author.

ALSO FROM INFINITY PUBLISHING

Dark Haunted Day is William P. Robertson's second collection of macabre tales. As the title indicates, ghost stories are the focus here. A gallant battlefield ghost, a malicious college phantom, and two spectral husbands are just a few of the hobgoblins haunting this anthology. Again, the author selects such Pennsylvania settings as Gettysburg, Mansfield, and the ever-spooky McKean County for his action. To add variety, a hunting horror story, a psychological thriller, and a Kinzua Viaduct death tale prey on the reader's imagination. Characters range from kids to the elderly, and all get their share of scares. To order an autographed copy of Dark Haunted Day, send $15.27 (postpaid) to William P. Robertson, P.O. Box 293, Duke Center, PA 16729. Make checks payable to the author. For more information about Bill's writing, e-mail him at buccobill@mail.usachoice.net.

Dark Haunted Day

More Tales of Terror
by
William P. Robertson